DEMANDING DISCORD

FIRE WITCHES OF SALEM
BOOK EIGHT

CARRIE PULKINEN

This is a work of fiction. Names, characters, places, and incidents are either the product of the author's imagination or are used fictitiously, and any resemblance to actual persons, living or dead, business establishments, events, or locales is entirely coincidental.

Demanding Discord

ISBN: 978-1-957253-46-6

CHAPTER 1

CINDER

Heat engulfed me like an electric blanket. I lay on my side, the warmth taming the excruciating ache in my muscles, and I snuggled into it, squeezing my eyes shut tightly and hoping to Hecate it was all just a wicked bad dream.

If it wasn't...well, that meant I had just killed two people, and that was *so very* not like me.

Sure, I battled the beasties that crossed into our realm whenever the occasion occurred, but they were just that...beasties. Tiny fae with razor teeth, who were as annoying as mosquitoes. Vampire ghouls with nothing but blood on their minds. Gnomes, ogres, and the occasional lower-level demon slipped through, but they didn't possess the brain power to hold a conversation and none of them presented a fully human form.

Killing the rhino motel clerk hadn't fazed me much. He was more intelligent than anything that had crossed to my side of the veil, but he was still a vile, disgusting beast who'd planned to kill and eat me. I'd acted in self-defense. I didn't need to feel bad about that.

What I'd done to Bedlam and Seraphine was also self-defense. So...why did I feel so rotten about it?

My shoulder ached from lying on it, so I adjusted my position. Something long and hard pressed into my butt cheek, and I popped my eyes open. I lay in complete darkness, and—aside from the sound of Discord breathing—utter silence.

Wait. If that was my demon wrapping me in warmth, that meant the hard thing pressed against my butt was his...

"Discord!" I shot to sitting and turned toward him. "Seriously?"

He didn't respond, so I lit a fireball, illuminating his form. He lay on his side, his eyes closed, and that rod I'd felt on my ass...?

It was the hilt of the dagger strapped to his thigh. *Whew.*

Although, after the kiss we'd shared by the river, I didn't know whether to be relieved or disappointed that his soldier wasn't saluting my presence.

Relieved, Cin. Definitely relieved. Sheesh.

I let out a breath and rose, taking in my surroundings. Red crystals in the rocky walls reflected my firelight, and an orange glow from the moon outside peeked around the massive boulder blocking the exit to the... Were we inside a cave? My backpack lay on the ground—apparently, I'd been using it as a pillow—and as I picked it up, Discord finally stirred.

He sucked in a sharp breath and pushed himself to sitting. "Cinder?"

"I'm here, though I'm not sure where *here* is." I sat next to him, still holding on to a flame. "What happened?"

"Your sisters summoned me after our battle. Are you okay?" He gently touched my chin, turning my head from side to side.

So it wasn't all a dream. Damn.

"I'm fine." I took two candles from my bag and lit them. "Where are we?"

"We're in a cave two miles from where we left Seraphine." He scrubbed his hands down his face. "You passed out the moment you dragged me away from the summoning."

Surprise lifted my brows. "You carried me two miles?"

He tilted his head, stretching his neck. "I had to. Seraphine had begun to stir."

"She's not dead?" A brick dropped from my chest to my stomach, and my mouth hung open.

"Sadly, no. Do you have any food in your bag? My body requires sustenance."

"Yeah. Let me see." I rummaged through the contents, finding two bars that resembled granola. I handed him one and unwrapped the other before shoving half of it into my mouth. It tasted smoky and slightly bitter, not at all what I was expecting, but not too terrible. I chewed, some kind of nut crunching between my teeth as I pondered our predicament.

Seraphine was alive. I wasn't sure how to feel about that. On one hand, it brought my body count down by one, which was a good thing. On the other, that meant she'd be extra pissed and would no doubt come after us as soon as she was able.

I think I preferred the higher body count.

"How close are we to Hecate's temple?" I took another bite and washed it down with stinky water, wrinkling my nose as I swallowed. I would never complain about the taste of Salem tap water again.

"A few miles out." Discord's expression darkened, his eyes tightening. "I have an unsettling feeling about it, though."

I took another sip of sulfur water and handed him the bottle. "This entire ordeal is unsettling. Could you be more specific?"

"I don't believe Hecate will be in her temple. You

found it too easily." He handed me the empty bottle and rose. "The seer had been scrying for years to no avail, yet you found the goddess within minutes. That doesn't make sense."

I bristled, my ego taking a hit. "After everything we've been through, now you're questioning my abilities?"

"Not at all. If any mortal witch could locate her, it would be you." He offered his hand. "You are the most amazing woman I have ever met."

Ignoring his last comment, I shoved the bottle into my backpack and accepted the gesture, letting him tug me to my feet. "Maybe she's ready to be found. And anyway, you helped me. Maybe the seer just needed to channel a Prince of Hell."

I tried to pull from his grasp, but he tightened his grip as we stood there, face to face, the intensity in his eyes making my stomach flutter. He was silent for a beat...two...three, and the fluttering rose to my chest.

"You saved my life." He sandwiched my hand between both of his, the warmth of his grip and the sincerity in his eyes making my breath catch.

"I didn't have much of a choice." My body drifted toward him of its own volition, the magnetism between us getting stronger with every battle we survived. "If you die, I die."

"You'd have saved me even if we weren't bound."

His gaze slid to my lips, and my heart raced. "As I would save you."

My mouth suddenly felt drier than the Mohave. "I'm a light witch. It's what we do." I licked my chapped lips, tugging my hand again. This time, he let me go.

I stepped away and grabbed my backpack, willing my hormones to calm the eff down. The urge to throw myself into his arms and let him ravish me right there on the cave floor overwhelmed me…but getting it on with a demon was the last thing I needed to worry about… Right now, anyway.

Honestly, if he hadn't kissed me by the river, I wouldn't be thinking about it at all. That kiss though… Damn.

He let out a little grunt, narrowing his eyes as I strapped on my backpack.

"We should get moving before someone figures out where we are." I leaned a shoulder against the giant rock blocking the cave entrance and pushed. It didn't budge. Of course it didn't. The damn thing was taller than me and probably weighed a ton, but I needed to get out of this confined, *private* space before I said *eff it all* and let my hormones take control.

"Or we could finish what we started on the river-bank." He rested a hand on the rock above my shoulder and leaned toward me, his smoldering gaze making my traitorous stomach flutter again.

"Not a chance." I pressed both palms against the boulder, shoving with all my bodyweight and ignoring the desire unfurling in my chest.

A strange look contorted his features for half a second, as if I'd physically slapped him, but he recovered and smirked. "This might be the only chance you get."

"I'm good with those odds." I flashed a tight-lipped smile and crossed my arms.

He inhaled deeply. "Your scent betrays you. I can smell your desire."

You have no idea... No doubt, my pheromones flared again at that animalistic statement, but I deflected and forced out a dry laugh. "We are not doing the deed on the cave floor." A girl had to have standards, right?

He arched a brow, mischief dancing in his eyes. "I could brace you against the wall."

Hecate on a highwire. Wouldn't that be something? If I kept my shirt on, maybe the rocks wouldn't chafe too badly. My backpack could act as a buffer too. He was definitely strong enough to hold me up, and we could... *Whoa. Slow your roll, Cin.*

Seriously, get a grip.

The sly grin on his lips told me I'd just turned the dial on whatever my desire smelled like to full blast. He took another deep breath, the knowing look in his eyes making me feel naked, even though I was fully clothed.

And Hecate knew I wouldn't mind getting naked with the man. He was packing quite the package, but... *Standards, Cin. You have standards.* "We're not doing it in a cave. End of story. Now, will you please move this rock so we can be on our way?"

"You don't deny the attraction."

I pressed my lips into a hard line. No. No, I did not. "That's not the point."

He gave me one more smirk and waved his hand in front of the boulder. When nothing happened, he cut his gaze toward me for half a second. I tried not to react, but damn. If he'd done his dematerializing trick to get us inside, and now we were trapped, I would become the unhappiest little camper he'd ever seen.

Closing his eyes, he took a deep breath. His muscles tensed, his nostrils flaring as he tried again. He waved his hand back and forth, his fingers curling into a claw, his exertion evident by the tendons protruding from his neck. He huffed, waving his arm three more times, and finally, it disappeared.

The memory of passing through the partially formed wall back at the palace had my feet moving before my brain had the chance to send the command. I darted through the opening and pressed my back against the outer wall, jerking my head side to side, searching for signs of an impending ambush. The coast seemed clear. For now.

Discord joined me outside the cave, and the

boulder blocking the entrance rematerialized. He winced and rubbed his chest. "Using magic has never affected me like this. Do you feel it too?"

I could tell it took a toll on him. Whether it was through our bond or just from his body language, I couldn't say. I didn't want to know. "Unless witches are using an inborn power like fire, magic always depletes our vim."

"It's unpleasant."

"That it is." I pushed from the wall and peered at our surroundings. We stood on a ledge deep in the canyon, about six feet above the acid river. Sheer cliffs rose all around, and steam hovered on the surface of the stream.

We could clamber our way down, but unless there was an invisible ladder around, we'd still be stuck at the bottom of the ravine. We had definitely ventured past the touristy part of the canyon. "How do we get out?"

"Normally, I'd bend space and drop us in front of the temple. But with the way my powers are waning..." He gestured to the jagged wall soaring twenty yards above us. "We'll have to climb."

I craned my neck, squinting in the glowing orange moonlight. The wall went straight up. No little trails or gradual inclines to make the feat even slightly easier. I'd visited the rock-climbing gym in Salem more than a few times, and fighting off ghouls and fae mosquitoes kept me in decent shape, but damn, that would be a long ascent.

"It's a good thing I'm not afraid of heights," I said. "Should we walk a ways and see if there's an easier spot to climb?"

"It doesn't get easier for miles in either direction." He rested a hand on a bulging rock. "Grab on here. The soles of your boots should grip the protrusions and recesses."

"I know how to climb." I wiped my sweaty palms on my pants. "I've just never done it without a rope."

"Ladies first." He stepped away from the wall, his gaze flowing down my body before returning to my eyes.

I fought a grin and grabbed the rock, hauling myself up the first three feet. "You just want to look at my butt, don't you?"

"The view is quite nice."

I glanced down, and he flashed a crooked smile, arching a brow in appreciation of the junk in my trunk.

"Are all demons horndogs, or is it just you?" I found another foothold and pushed, using my leg strength to reach above and grab another protruding rock. Whether my heart was pounding from the physical exertion or the flirtatious demon, I couldn't say. Probably both.

"I haven't been with a woman in over four hundred years." He hauled himself up and followed as

I climbed. "The kiss we shared has awakened a beast inside me."

Good goddess. I didn't dare look down, but I could imagine his hungry expression, the fire in his eyes as he prowled toward me, the deftness of his hands and tongue. *Whew.* In all fairness, it had been a while for me too. Not four hundred years, but long enough to make his advances sound way more appealing than they should, especially in our current predicament.

And that beast he claimed I'd awakened... Sweet spirits and spells, how I would love to meet him. *Gah! Concentrate, Cin.* I was only halfway to the top, and my muscles were screaming with the exertion.

My thighs and shoulders burned, and my fingers felt like I'd scraped them against the steaming blacktop on the school playground. If I could focus on those physical sensations, maybe I could ignore the heat pooling in my nether region.

Twenty feet to go. I peered up and found an indentation in the stone just big enough to fit my fingers in. I grabbed on and pulled, gripping the wall with the soles of my boots. My pulse thrummed, my breathing growing shallow as I hauled myself up.

Sharp pain sliced through my index finger, as if it had been stabbed and wrenched out of the socket at the same time.

"Son of a bitch!" I yanked my hand out and lost my footing. My left hand gripped a piece of obsidian protruding from the rock, but the surface was too slick. My fingers slipped, and I fell backward, Hans Gruber from *Die Hard* style.

Please don't let me land in the acid was the only thought in my mind. Time seemed to slow as I plummeted and stared up at the weird moon hanging in the cloudless sky.

Discord gripped my forearm, stopping my fall, but my body swung, slamming into the wall with a *thunk*. My head smacked the rocks, and my vision swam. Thankfully, instinct made me latch on to his arm too, because his grip slipped. I caught his wrist half a nanosecond before I continued my unwelcome descent, and his fingers encircled my arm, locking us together.

I blinked my vision back into focus and scrambled around to find something to hold on to. "I'm okay," I lied, my breathless voice giving me away.

"Climb onto my back," he said. "I'll carry you out of the ravine."

"I said I'm okay." I tugged from his grasp and grabbed another rock, pulling myself above him.

A spark of annoyance lit in my chest, fueling my adrenaline. I climbed faster than I had ever climbed before, muttering to myself the entire way up. Did he seriously just suggest a piggyback ride? To a strong, absolutely capable woman? To an elemental witch?

The good news was his ridiculous suggestion had

squelched any desire I'd felt toward him. Hopefully, he could smell that too.

And hopefully, I could get my emotions off this damn rollercoaster. My own mood swings were about to give me whiplash, but I blamed that on all the trauma we'd endured since we arrived in Hell. It was enough to make anyone crack beneath the pressure. Not me, though. I refused to break.

A gnarled black tree stood at the top of the canyon, its twisted roots exposed and reaching downward, creating the perfect grip for the last few feet of my ascent.

"Don't," Discord shouted, but it was too late.

I grabbed a root, and an array of teeny, tiny spikes, no thicker than acupuncture needles, sank half a millimeter into my palm, making it itch like a flea-infested werewolf with mange.

Scrambling to the ground above, I army crawled onto the surface, took two deep breaths, and rose to my feet. My hand burned like the spikes had injected me with everything I could possibly be allergic to, but I ignored the pain, grinding my teeth as Discord pulled himself over the edge.

"First of all, you need to stop treating me like some damsel in distress." I flicked my wrist, fanning my burning hand.

Discord fought an amused grin. "Perhaps if you stopped putting yourself in distress, I would."

I opened my mouth, ready to insist he give examples, but I closed it again, ticking off the list of times he'd had to carry me in my mind. "I'm not a damsel."

He chuckled. "Noted. Would you like some help with your hand?"

I finally looked at my offending appendage, and Hecate have mercy. My index finger had swollen to the size of a sausage, and the skin on my palm had turned purple and pruney. "What the hell?"

He gingerly took my hand in his, turning it over and back again. "That tree is a thorny ash. Its sap causes burning, itching, and blisters."

"Fabulous. I caught herpes of the hand from a thorny ass tree." I bent my fingers and winced at the searing pain.

His brow furrowed. "Thorny *ash*. It also causes necrosis. Your finger, though. Did something bite you? The reaction reminds me of brimstone scorpion venom."

"Probably. That's why I fell." I slipped my backpack off one shoulder. "Let me see if I've got any healing herbs."

"No need." He lifted my other arm and ran his finger over the sigil. "I can help you, if you'll admit you are, once again, in distress." Amusement danced in his eyes, and I narrowed mine.

My gut reaction was to tell him hell no. I was stubborn, like most first-born daughters were, but the black blisters forming on my palm made me think better of it.

"Please fix me," I muttered.

He covered the sigil with his hand. "Are you in distress, sweet damsel witch?"

I sighed and shook my head. "Yes, Prince Pain In My Ass, I am in distress. I need my big, strong demon to use his magical healing ability to help me. Happy now?"

"Indeed." He closed his eyes and inhaled deeply. As he let out a slow breath, the invisible tether connecting us vibrated and heated. His magic seeped into my skin, spreading through my chest before cascading down my arm and gathering in my hand.

A flush of coolness spread over my palm, and the pain in my finger turned from razor sharp to a dull ache to nothing. The blisters disappeared, and the swelling faded as if I'd never been injured.

I stared at my hand in awe before looking into his eyes. "Thank you."

He bowed his head. "Taking care of you is my pleasure... Words I never dreamed I would utter to anyone."

Cue the flip-flopping stomach. Again.

Before I could even begin to form a response in my mind, he took my face in his hands and planted his mouth on mine, and yeah... I'll admit I melted a little.

Okay, a lot.

He just had these full, soft lips that fit over mine like they were made to kiss me, and his body... I couldn't help but lean into him, pressing my curves against his angles, parting my lips so he could swipe his tongue against mine.

All the blood in my brain plummeted below my navel, and I allowed myself to get lost in his embrace for a moment. A little longer. Longer still...

But this was wrong. He was a demon for Hecate's sake, and I was on a mission to survive Hell and find a way home.

I broke the kiss on a quick inhale and touched my fingers to my lips. They still tingled; his taste lingered on my tongue.

"Which..." I cleared my throat. "Which way to Hecate's temple?"

His eyes smoldered with an intensity I could barely stand, and that beast I'd supposedly awakened...? He was ready to devour me.

CHAPTER 2

DISCORD

Had we not been exposed in the open air, I could have taken her right there on the ground. I *should* have taken her inside the cave when I'd had the chance...kissed her then, at the very least.

I could smell her desire when I'd suggested we fornicate, and I had let a little magic slip, seeping discord into her psyche, attempting to loosen her rational thoughts and allow her emotions to guide her to me. Strangely, my attempt had brought clarity to her mind, and she'd handed me a firm no.

I could have pressed her, but trying to force Cinder to do anything she didn't want to would be an exercise in futility, which I had no desire to attempt. She would claim my attraction to her—my desire to protect and take care of her in every way—was due to the union placed on us against our will. That this longing I felt deep within my soul meant nothing...would be nothing when our marks were removed.

At first, I'd thought so as well. Now, I wasn't so sure.

"Why did you summon me?" I asked.

She furrowed her brows over her deep honey eyes. "You're kidding, right?"

"I am not."

She laughed dryly. "To find my parents...? Are you okay?"

I shook my head. "I know that."

Confusion contorted her features as she tilted her head. "Then why are you asking?"

"I mean why *me*? Why not Chaos or Mayhem? Why did you choose me?"

She frowned and shrugged. "I just picked a name from the list. Can we get moving? I'm feeling anxious out here in the open."

"The temple you described is on the outskirts of the barren land stretching out before us. This way." I rested my hand on the small of her back to indicate she should walk beside me. She matched my pace, her legs moving unhindered in her modern pants and boots.

"Was my mark at the top of the list? Is that why you chose me?" I asked, though I knew better. None of this was a coincidence.

"It was at the bottom, if you must know." Her face pinched as if she already sensed my assumptions.

"What made you skip to the bottom? You could have summoned either of my brothers just as easily."

She caught the corner of her bottom lip between her teeth and blinked five times before she answered, "I don't know. I guess the design of your sigil called to me. It felt like you were the one... The one who could help me, I mean."

I nodded. "It's kismet."

She cut a sideways glance. "It's a curse. A literal curse. If not for that, I wouldn't be here."

"Fair point," I said, and we continued our trek in silence.

Black rock stretched out before us in every direction, and humid heat clung to my skin. The scents of pungent sulfur and smoky, acrid tar hung in the damp air, growing stronger the farther we ventured into the abandoned wasteland.

"I don't believe the blood magic that joined us was accidental," I said.

She scoffed. "I definitely didn't do it on purpose."

"Perhaps not consciously," I said, "but the seer finishing the bond, your sisters summoning my brothers, you choosing my sigil out of the three... This is happening for a reason."

"And the reason is that you decided to curse my

bloodline." She crossed her arms, continuing to match my pace.

"It's more than that."

She shook her head adamantly. "It's not. Believe me."

"Your sisters found my brothers. I saw them when they attempted to summon me."

"They found them because I asked them to. I left a note for Ash to find if I didn't make it back home. It's not kismet or fate or even serendipity. They're following a plan—*my* plan—which I put into place before I summoned you."

"I felt their bonds. Three sisters for three brothers. Three powerful witches for three demon princes." How could she not see that fate had a hand in this?

"Let me stop you right there." She turned and held up a finger. "If Ash and Ember are getting it on with your brothers, that's none of my business. But this... these feelings we have for each other...? Magic fabricated them, and magic will undo them. Think about that before you decide you're horns-over-hooves in love with me or some other nonsense."

"Why you then?" I continued walking.

She followed by my side. "I'm the eldest daughter, the one who knew about the curse. It had to be me."

"Why no one before you? Your ancestors have been in peril for centuries, yet you were the first to try and right the situation."

"I don't know. You'd have to ask them."

"It's because everything is happening the way fate intended it to. We're meant to be together, and not even your silver tongue could convince me otherwise."

"Then we'll just have to agree to disagree." She lifted her arms and dropped them at her sides, the look on her face indicating the conversation was over.

I could have pressed her further...circled back to her admission that she chose me because it felt right...but I refrained. Once we found Hecate, the goddess would confirm that fate had woven this tapestry long before Cinder was born. Possibly before even I came into being. Then, she'd have no grounds to deny it.

Cinder was my soul bride, not because of an accident that led to a series of unfortunate events, but because she was meant to be mine.

We continued in silence, walking until nothing but rock, dappled with slick patches of obsidian, stretched out as far as I could see. Cinder wrinkled her nose, the tar and sulfur aromas no doubt offending her senses. The smell and thickness of the air began to offend mine as well.

The orange moon hung still in the sky, as always, providing no hint of how long we'd been on our journey. Months could have passed in the earthly realm, where here it had only been days. Then again, with time behaving the way it did in Hell, we could have been walking for months while only minutes passed in the other realm.

It was enough to drive a man insane, and that was by design, of course.

"Good goddess, it smells like broccoli and egg dog farts." Cinder waved a hand in front of her face. "Why would Hecate have a temple way out here?"

"She's an ancient goddess, who was worshipped long before Lucifer came into rule. This was her level of the Underworld until he took control of the realm. When he did, he claimed the eighth level as his kingdom because of the molten rivers. Building there, flourishing despite the destructive nature of magma, proved his unparalleled power."

She scoffed. "So it was a flex."

"If by that you mean a way for him to easily subjugate the denizens here, then yes. It was a flex."

"Figures. What level is this then? How can you tell when you enter a new one?"

"Crossing the ravine where we did brought us into the fifth level. This barren land was once the epicenter of the Underworld. It's where souls, escorted by Hecate and her psychopomps, would enter the realm before passing into their eternities."

"And let me guess. Lucifer razed it as his first flex."

I chuckled. "Not his first, but one of many."

"And still she fell for him. I don't get it."

"Trying to understand the thought process of deities is futile at best."

The terrain angled upward, and when we reached the top of the incline, a valley lay before us. Geysers of fire erupted from sulfurous craters, shooting toward the sky, intensifying the stench in the air. On the far side, a cave burrowed into the rock, and in the center of the valley, Hecate's original Underworld temple lay in ruins.

Made of black stone and obsidian, the once magnificent structure stood crumbling, its columns having toppled, its walls deteriorated after millennia of neglect. The triple moon, Hecate's sigil, barely showed through the layers of ash and dirt on the pediment, and a line of statues, now headless and limbless, lined the path toward the steps.

"Wow," Cinder said, her eyes wide with wonder. "I can't imagine our goddess living here. Not even part-time."

"Temples are structures where deities are worshipped, not where they reside." I took her hand and guided her down the path, the foreboding feeling that had unsettled me earlier growing stronger with each step.

"Where does she stay when she's in Hell, then?" She stopped at the first dismembered statue and examined it.

"Before she joined Lucifer's court, I do not know," I

said, studying her intently. She must have felt the same hesitation as I did. "After they coupled, she resided in the palace. I'm not sure if she spent nights in this realm at all before then."

Cinder rubbed her arms. "Do you feel that?"

"What do you feel?"

"Fresh magic. For an abandoned temple, it sure feels...alive." She took three more steps and paused to study the torso of a woman in a Grecian robe. "She must be here."

I caught her hand before she could continue up the path. "Are you sure it's Hecate's energy that you feel? The vibration I sense is too low. Focus on it."

She chuckled. "Did you just ask me to do a vibe check?"

"If vibe is short for vibration, then yes. The energy feels demonic."

Closing her eyes, she inhaled two deep breaths. "Everything has felt demonic since the moment I got here. I can't tell the difference anymore."

"We should leave."

"And go where? So far, this is the only lead we've got, and if there is even the slightest chance Hecate is hiding in there, we have to check it out."

I was loath to continue this journey. Whatever awaited us inside would not be the benevolent goddess Cinder hoped to find, but—against my better judgment—I agreed. We had no other option. "Proceed with caution."

"Always." She crept forward, one hand resting on the dagger at her hip, the other stretched outward as if she were feeling the air for magic. Her arm hairs stood on end, and tension rolled off her in waves. Instinct told her something was awry, but she chose to ignore it...a dangerous decision.

I followed her as she continued toward the temple, my stomach sinking further with each step. "Why do we assume Hecate is in the Underworld? If she were that angry with Lucifer, would she not have left the realm?"

Cinder turned toward me. "I don't think she can leave."

"She's the original psychopomp. Of course she can."

She pressed her lips into a line and shook her head. "Not without the amulet. Seraphine told me her magic is stuck inside it."

I stopped abruptly, grabbing Cinder's hand before she could ascend the steps. "What do you mean?"

"Apparently, that amulet was a token of their love. Lucifer infused it with his power to send beings across the veil at whim, and Hecate gave up her power of resurrection. Neither of them can send anyone to other realms...including themselves, I assume."

Annoyance twisted in my chest. "Why are you just now telling me this?"

"I've been a little distracted." She shrugged.

"We cannot survive this quest while withholding information from each other."

"Now you know how I've felt since the moment I met you." She tugged from my grasp. "I wasn't withholding on purpose. You almost died. Then I almost died. Then you kissed me. Twice. Cut me some slack."

I ground my teeth. She made a fair point. I hadn't been the most forthcoming with her thus far, but our situation had changed. My feelings for this feisty woman had changed.

What irked me now was the fact that Seraphine, a mere witch, knew the true purpose of the amulet when I did not. If I had known the symbolism, the reason for its creation, I never would have wagered it all those centuries ago.

"You are forgiven," I said, "and, technically, you kissed me the first time."

She rolled her eyes and smiled. "We're even then."

"I promise to divulge any and all important information to you from this point forward," I said. "Will you pledge the same?"

"Of course." Her eyes widened as if the speed of her reply surprised her. "Like I said, I wasn't keeping it a secret on purpose. Can we go in now?"

"Allow me to en—"

She climbed the steps and disappeared inside.

CHAPTER 3

CINDER

Clutching a dagger in my right hand, I crept into the temple, darkness engulfing me the moment I crossed the threshold, plunging me into an inky blackness unlike anything I'd ever experienced. I held the blade in front of my face, but I might as well have been blindfolded. No light seeped inside, so it didn't even reflect a faint glint.

I lit a fireball in my hand, expecting to illuminate at least a quarter of the room, but my flames barely penetrated the darkness. I could only see about a foot in every direction, and the first hint of panic flushed my veins like ice water.

"How good is your night vision?" I turned around, being careful not to move out of my spot, expecting my demon's rumbly voice to break the silence. I heard nothing.

"Discord?" My pulse thrummed, and my throat thickened. I sheathed my dagger and extended my arm, shuffling slowly in the direction from which I'd entered, searching for the exit or a wall...not that I expected to find a light switch. I just needed to ground myself, because standing in an empty void had me nauseated and hyperventilating.

"Discord," I shouted. "Where are you?"

Had the man not bothered to follow me inside? He'd seemed convinced coming here was a waste of time, so maybe he'd decided to let me find out for myself. Alone.

I swallowed the thickness from my throat and shuffled a few more steps toward...what? A hellmouth? A pool of acid? A pit of despair? My sense of direction had been snuffed out along with my vision. I thought I'd been heading toward the exit, but as I crept forward, sliding one foot in front of the other, testing the viability of the floor before shifting my weight, it seemed I was going deeper into the temple.

"This isn't funny, Discord. Get your ass in here." The darkness swallowed my words as if I were shouting into a pillow. My heart beat like a hummingbird had taken flight in my chest, and that pillow I was screaming into...? It just ripped open and filled my mouth with a wad of cotton.

I sucked in a deep, shaky breath...two...three...and tried to get a handle on my anxiety. Discord had felt uneasy about coming here. If he'd thought it was dangerous to come inside, he wouldn't have sent me in alone. We were a team, whether I liked it or not, and he wouldn't have risked my life to prove a point.

Sure, he was arrogant and broody, but he wanted to survive this as much as I did. He needed me alive, plain and simple. What wasn't so simple...?

My feelings for him. Every time he swore we were meant to be together, my stomach did a little dance inside my abdomen. This wasn't the time, place, or lifetime for me to be falling for a demon, but one thing was certain... He wouldn't have sent me in here alone any more than I would have sent him, and I did *not* like the implications of that fact.

Did he get ambushed the second I stepped inside? Did he use magic that drained him enough to make it impossible to walk? I was still alive and kicking, so no one had obliterated him yet. Or...

Was I still alive?

Discord had described the dark prison as a sensory deprivation chamber. Was this pitch-black darkness my new eternity? Was I in prison? Was I dead?

No. No way was I dead. If someone died in Hell, their soul was obliterated. I wouldn't be able to think, much less panic about my predicament.

This was Hecate's temple. Of course it would be magical. This was some sort of test I needed to pass before I could find her. It had to be.

"No problem, Cin. You've got this." I crept forward blindly, swinging my arm from side to side so I didn't bump into anything. I tapped my toes on the ground before each step to make sure it hadn't fallen away in front of me. The hummingbird in my chest flew upward to beat its wings in my throat, and I did my best to take deep, slow breaths.

A menacing growl sounded to my left, breaking the silence, and instinct took over. I chucked a fireball in the direction of the sound. Yes, I knew witch fire didn't hurt demons in Hell, but like I said...instinct. As it turned out, not hurting my adversary was the least of my problems.

The fireball hit something, and a flash of light nearly blinded me. It bounced off whatever it hit and hurled toward me. I raised my hand, ready to call the flames back, but a crashing sound to my right distracted me. I spun and stumbled, catching myself on a stone ledge. My fingers plunged into something thick and wet. *Yuck.*

The fireball hit the wall and erupted. A massive stone bowl stood on an ornate pedestal, and whatever it contained was flammable. *Highly* flammable. Heat blasted my skin, the wind whipping my hair back as the flames finally illuminated the room.

A small channel descended from the vat of fire, and flames licked their way down it, igniting smaller bowls and torches as they passed. That wet stuff I'd plunged my hand into? It was oil, and thank the goddess I was fireproof.

My fingers burst into flames, and I held up my hand, spinning in a circle and taking in my surroundings as the fire consumed the oil on my skin. The walls soared thirty feet high, purple gems embedded in the stone glittering in the firelight, and a twenty-foot statue of the goddess rose between two dancing flames. She wore a flowing gown and held a fiery staff, and two dogs sat at her side, gazing up at her.

My breath came out in a rush, and I pressed my hand to my chest as I bowed before her image. Goosebumps pricked on my skin, the fine hairs on my arms and the back of my neck standing on end. Never had I ever been this close to the actual goddess herself.

Sure, she'd come to me in dreams. She'd answered our prayers and sent us messages when we'd performed rituals and asked for her blessing, but this... This was some next-level, once-in-a-lifetime, no-one-has-been-here-and-made-it-out-alive shit.

Why hadn't I thought to bring an offering?

"Oh!" I swung my backpack to my front and grabbed a handful of the herbs I'd taken from the seer before laying them at the statue's feet. "Goddess, please accept this token. I am your humble disciple. Blessed be."

I repositioned my backpack and buckled it at my waist. "Hecate? Are you here?"

A torch ignited on the far wall, illuminating a doorway to the next chamber. I glanced from it to the main entrance and swallowed the lemon-sized lump in my throat. Darkness blanketed both passages. I couldn't see what lay beyond either threshold, and I chewed the inside of my cheek as I contemplated my next move.

"Discord?" I called. Silence answered.

Where the eff was he? My stomach soured, but I focused my gaze on the doorway to the next chamber. I was here. Discord wasn't, and no matter the reason for his absence, I had to push through. I didn't need his help; I could do this alone.

Another growl rumbled from behind me, spurring me into motion. I strode to the passage, pausing for a breath before crossing into the darkness.

I half-expected the chamber to light up like it had motion sensors. Unfortunately, it did not, so I lit another fireball in my hand. I could still only see about a foot in any direction, so I slowly turned and shuffled toward what I hoped was the wall. A torch hung from a sconce, and I took it, lighting the end.

A bowl of oil rested on a pedestal beneath the sconce, so I tapped the fiery end of the torch against it. This room had a similar, though much smaller, setup as the main chamber, and the flames licked down an oily channel, lighting more bowls and torches until warm light illuminated the entire space.

I liked it better when it was dark.

Long and narrow, the chamber stretched on for at least fifty yards before plunging into darkness, which was impossible. The temple was big, but not *that* big. Unless I'd just stepped into Dr. Who's TARDIS, it had to be an optical illusion.

Mirrors ten feet tall lined the walls, and red sigils etched into the glass glowed along the top of each one. I crept forward and faced the first one, my distorted reflection bouncing off the mirror behind me and creating infinite Cinders in both directions.

Something growled from the entry, and I whirled toward it. A massive, jet-black German shepherd crouched, its lips peeled back over pointy teeth.

Doggo rule number one: Never make eye contact with an angry canine. I knew that, but it didn't stop me from locking my gaze on its glittering yellow eyes.

"Who's a good boy?" I asked in the softest, gentlest voice I could muster. My question earned me another growl.

I held up my hands and inched backward, deeper into the tunnel. "You're Hecate's guardian, right? I'm a witch, her faithful disciple. Have you seen her?"

The dog's growl grew deeper, rumbling in its chest, and it took two steps toward me.

I slowly reached for the dagger strapped to my thigh. "Please don't make me be the reason another dog dies."

My fingers curled around the handle. The dog lunged. Dammit.

I drew my blade and swiped at the fluffy guy's neck before falling backward onto my butt. Sharp pain shot from my tailbone to my skull, and I gasped. The dog was gone.

I jerked my head from side to side and scrambled onto my hands and knees. "What the actual eff?"

Still clutching my dagger, I rose to my feet and rubbed my lower back. Had I just obliterated one of Hecate's beloved hounds? "Dear goddess, please forgive me."

A deep, menacing, masculine laugh echoed in the chamber, and I spun toward the sound. The same dog...or maybe its twin...crouched, its weight on its haunches, ready to leap.

"Was that you?" I held the dagger toward the animal, and it growled.

A disembodied whistle sounded from behind it, and its ears perked half a second before it attacked. I lunged to the side, trying to avoid its razor-sharp teeth, and I crashed into a mirror, shattering it. Shards of magical glass rained onto the floor, and the glowing sigils on the mirror across from it dimmed, turning ashy gray before disappearing as if they'd never been etched into it at all.

The temple groaned in protest like it had felt the

mirror break in its soul. And the dog...? Gone again. If it was really even there to begin with.

I gazed at my reflection in another mirror, tilting my head and furrowing my brow as an idea wriggled into my consciousness. The glass felt cool beneath my fingertips, and I blew from my throat, clouding the surface before drawing the fire witch sigil, a triangle inside a triquetra, in the fog.

The menacing, masculine laugh echoed through the chamber again, making my muscles crawl beneath my skin. "Whoever you are, you don't belong here," I said.

"Neither do you." The voice sounded like it came from everywhere around me *and* from inside my head.

In the mirror's reflection, a shadow passed behind me. Heart pounding, I spun, facing the opposite mirror, and the image of Tumult wearing crimson fatigues, so dark they were nearly black, appeared behind me. I gasped and spun again, slashing my dagger right and left.

He wasn't there. Neither physically in the room, nor in the opposite mirror's image. I turned again, and there he was, standing behind my shoulder.

"How the hell...?" I stepped closer to the mirror, narrowing my eyes at the demon. I could feel his presence as if he really loomed behind me: the lower vibration of energy, the shifting of the air as if someone moved, the hairs on the back of my neck standing on end, reacting to...nothing, it seemed.

"Where are Discord and Hecate?" I glared at Tumult, tightening my grip on the dagger.

"Do you truly believe I would give you that information?" He inclined his chin, looking down his nose at me.

His condescension irked me, so I laid my magic on thick. "I do, because I know you want to."

"You know nothing," he growled.

"Lucifer is volatile, ready to explode at any minute, and do you know why?" I didn't wait for him to answer. "Because he wants Hecate back. Imagine his surprise and appreciation when you return to the palace, not with my head, but with his one true love."

He blinked, his brows drawing together as if the idea intrigued him. Good. My persuasion magic was working.

"Think about it," I said. "The whole reason he wants Discord and me dead is because Hecate left him. Bringing him our skulls won't appease him for long. He needs his woman by his side."

He laughed again, deeply and heartily, throwing his head back as if I were the funniest person he'd ever met. "Foolish witch."

My mouth tightened. Maybe my magic wasn't working. "You're starting to sound like a movie villain.

Either come out here and fight me or skedaddle. I've got a goddess to find."

"Revenge is more satisfying than any woman's touch. Lucifer shall have your heads."

I rolled my eyes. "Tell me you suck in the intimacy department without telling me you suck."

Confusion contorted his features for a second before he worked out the meaning of my words. "You dare mock Tumult, Crown Prince of Hell?"

Now it was my turn to laugh. "Crown prince, eh? Someone thinks highly of himself. How does that even work when the king is an immortal god? It sounds to me like you're fighting to be by his side, to be his servant, to win second place...and we all know what second place is."

He arched a brow, clearly not getting the reference.

"It's the first loser, dipshit." I turned on my heel and strode toward the next mirror.

Tumult whistled, and the black dog appeared before me. I barely had time to call him a good boy before he sprang. I threw up my arms, preparing for impact, shielding my face from his vicious maw with one hand, and jabbing the dagger at his chest with the other.

Wind whipped my air backward as the dog passed through me and disappeared.

My heart took up residence in my throat with the attack, so I sucked in a deep breath and swallowed hard. The dog wasn't real. Or...maybe it was real, but it wasn't *really* there. Tumult was creating it like a hologram, sending it into the room with some kind of projection magic.

And if the dog wasn't really there, the demon wasn't either.

I turned to the next mirror. Tumult's image smiled wickedly back at me, but...why didn't *I* have a reflection?

I spun to the opposite one. No reflection there either. I stepped to the next one in the line. Nothing. Either I'd turned into a vampire or Tumult was messing with my mind.

The dog snarled and charged. I stood my ground, resting one hand on my hip as it approached. I'd be lying if I said I wasn't at least a little scared the beast would be solid this time, but I wasn't about to give the infuriating demon the satisfaction of watching me flinch.

The beastie passed through me once again, and I let out a relieved breath. The dog didn't have to die this time.

"Is that all you've got?" I straightened and strolled to the next mirror. No reflection once again. My stomach soured as I leaned toward it, and I pressed my fingertips against the glass. The twin panes reflected each other into infinity, but it looked as if the dog wasn't the only being who wasn't really here. It seemed I wasn't either.

Tumult strode into the reflection, a million demons stretching on forever in the glass, their smiles menacing, their gazes wicked.

Wait. Last time, I only saw him in the one mirror. If he was reflecting back on forth now, that meant he…

I whirled around, and his fist hit my jaw.

Pain exploded on the side of my face, and I careened backward, into the mirror. It shattered like the other one, and the walls groaned with its demise. A sharp, stabbing sensation throbbed in my left triceps, and I yanked out the offending piece of glass before lunging at the demon.

He disappeared…because of course he did…and my momentum hurled me into the opposite mirror, shattering it too. Dirt rained from the ceiling above, and I had to wonder if maybe these mirrors really were pieces of the temple's soul.

Or of Hecate's. Goddess, I hoped not.

I clutched my dagger in one hand, held a shard of glass in the other, and turned in a circle. "Only a coward does drive-bys. Are you afraid of a little, mortal witch?"

He landed a punch to my gut as he came fully into view. I doubled over, sucking in a breath before straightening and jabbing my dagger upward. The blade hit his chin, penetrating the skin and slicing into his tongue.

I yanked it out, and blood poured from his mouth as he roared. Talons extended from his fingertips. He swiped his claws at my throat. I jerked away before he could rip out my windpipe, but the tips of his razor talons nicked my neck, stinging like papercuts.

"Son of a banshee!" Blood rolled into my cleavage.

Tumult cracked his neck, and the edges of his wound stitched themselves back together. I lunged, aiming my dagger at his heart. He knocked me aside like I was nothing more than a pesky fly.

My butt hit the ground, my tailbone screaming at me to stop—for the love of the goddess—landing on my ass.

I scrambled to my feet and feinted with my right hand, drawing his attention to the dagger while jabbing the shard of mirror into his chest. The sharp edge sliced into my palm with the impact, and blood pooled both in my hand and on his shirt.

He flinched, surprise widening his eyes, but my makeshift weapon obviously had not gone in deep enough to obliterate him. I swung the dagger, ready to sink it into his heart, but he recovered, grabbing my wrist and wrenching the blade from my hand.

Tumult clutched my throat and hurled me toward the entrance. My back smacked the stone wall, and my breath whooshed from my lungs. Intense, prickly pain radiated from the small of my back, down both legs, and, my vision swimming, I slid to the floor.

The demon dragged me up by my hair and pressed the dagger to my throat.

Fantastic. I was to be annihilated by my own blade.

I didn't have the strength left in me to fight, so I turned on my magic full-blast one last time. "You know Discord will be obliterated the second you kill me, right? You'll never get his skull."

He sneered. "I'll be quick."

I was about to launch into a persuasive speech about how he'd need us both together to be *that* quick, but my thoughts were interrupted by the most melodic, beautiful, *guttural roar* I had ever heard.

Discord burst into the room, his nostrils flaring, his eyes wild with malice. Tumult shoved me aside, and as his image began to fade out, his corporeal form slipping back onto whatever plane he had come from, Discord grabbed him by the throat and yanked him out of the room.

I tried to follow, but a wall materialized where the doorway should have been. With an echoing bang, the firelight extinguished, plunging me into darkness, the sigils glowing on the edges of a single mirror providing the only light in the room.

CHAPTER 4

DISCORD

"What have you done to her?" I slammed Tumult into the wall and pressed my forearm against his throat, blocking his air supply. He wheezed, so I loosened my hold enough for him to speak.

"Her who? You'll have to be more specific." He plunged his talons into my stomach and jerked them upward, searing pain shocking my body and making me freeze.

He pulled them out, and I stumbled back, clutching my abdomen, lest my innards attempted to spill onto the floor. I focused on the jagged tears stretching across my stomach, willing my energy to gather in the wound and speed my healing, but I'd used too much power helping Cinder after our climb.

Then, the temple had blocked my entrance, and I'd

used more magic and brute force in my attempt to get inside. I was, as Cinder would say, spent.

Tumult tilted his head, walking a circle around me like a hellcat prowling, toying with its prey. He glanced toward the wall I'd created where the doorway used to be. "I see Lucifer didn't strip you of all your powers. I am sure that took a toll, though, did it not?"

I pulled my hand away, my palm covered in blood, and I tried to straighten. A flash of sharp, intense pain took my breath, and part of my intestine slipped through the wound, protruding from the gash in my shirt. A grunt was all I could offer my adversary in response as I pushed the offending innards back inside where they belonged.

"Stuck in your human form. Using any type of magic drains your energy. You require sleep." He chuckled. "Because you believe witches are more important than your duty as a prince, Lucifer decided to let you feel what it's like to be one."

"I am no witch." I squeezed the sides of my wound together, aiding my body's repair.

He waved a hand, my blood on his talons glinting in the firelight. "You've lost Lucifer's favor. You may as well be *human*." His lip curled on the last word.

"Perhaps he stripped my powers because it was the only way you had a chance at beating me." I straightened, my abdominal muscles finally healing enough to hold my insides in. "If I had my full strength, you would already be dead."

"You—" He faltered, his brows slamming down over dark crimson eyes.

I used his momentary distraction to my advantage and charged. My body crashed into his, and I pinned his arms to his sides as I tackled him. The back of his head hit the stone floor with a sickening *thwack*, and his rancid breath left his lungs in a rush.

Rising to my knees, I slammed my fist into his face, bloodying his nose. He rolled, latching his taloned hands onto my arms and throwing me onto my back. I caught his fist before it made contact with the side of my head and wrenched his arm outward, twisting and dislocating his elbow. His joint popped, echoing in the chamber, and I twisted harder...until bone protruded from his skin.

He wailed and stumbled to his feet, pinning me with a fiery glare before his corporeal form blinked out, his essence slipping into the plane between Hell and the ether.

I rose and spun, my senses heightened, searching for sounds or the stink of his breath...anything to alert me to his presence on this plane. The crackling of the fire was all I heard. My pulse thrummed, and I took shallow breaths, my gaze darting around the room as I slipped a dagger from my thigh holster.

I sensed nothing.

My stomach sank. Had he returned to the next chamber to continue his assault on Cinder? If I dematerialized the wall I'd created, my strength would diminish even more. I barely had enough in me to fight as I stood.

"You'll never earn a place by Lucifer's side," I said. "There will always be someone better than you."

A low growl rumbled to my left. Good. I had his attention.

"In my absence, he chose Ruin," I continued my taunt. "He never believed you could fulfill the role."

"When I bring him both your heads, he will understand my worth." The energy shifted in front of me, and Tumult's arm in demonic form jutted from the next plane to swipe at my shoulder.

I side-stepped his advance, but he clocked me in the jaw with his other hand before fading again. Pain lurched upward to my temple, but I didn't give him the satisfaction of witnessing a reaction.

"Lucifer created *me* to stand by his side." I tightened my grip on the knife. "Even if you could beat me, you would never live up to his standards. You will eternally be nothing more than second best."

Footsteps pounded on the stone, Tumult's form slipping onto this plane as he charged toward me, claws and teeth bared. I parried, sinking my blade into his shoulder before yanking it out and using his momentum to propel him across the room. He crashed into a dog statue at Hecate's feet, knocking it from its stone base and breaking it into three pieces.

The temple groaned as if it had felt pain. Dust rained from the ceiling.

Tumult sat up, clutching his injured shoulder and slipping between planes. "You can't beat me. My power makes it impossible for you to catch me."

"Your power is bred in cowardice." I cast my gaze upward. Fine cracks lined the columns supporting the ceiling. "You hide like a child rather than fight like a man."

"I am no coward." He appeared three feet to my left, spreading his arms in welcome. "If a fight is what you want, come and get me. I'm here."

I lunged, lashing out with my knife and striking at his chest.

He disappeared in a wispy mist, his deep laugh sounding behind me. "Or am I here?"

I turned and lunged once more. Again, my knife passed through nothing more than mist.

"Perhaps I am here." He appeared at the foot of Hecate's statue. "Or here." A second image of Tumult formed atop her head.

"Boo," he said, his rancid breath heating my ear half a second before he plunged his claws deep into my back...so deep they protruded from my chest, racking my entire body with agony.

I coughed, and blood poured from my mouth. He

had penetrated a lung, missing my heart by less than an inch.

"I'll take your head now." He shoved me to my knees and wrenched the knife from my grasp.

"Only a coward takes out their enemy from behind," I spat and wiped my mouth with the back of my hand.

He grabbed my hair, jerking my head back as he moved into view. "I hope she was worth it."

He raised his arm, prepared to sever my head. He was not prepared, however, for what I did next. Simple punctures healed much more quickly than jagged tears, and my lung had already mended.

I sucked in a breath and swept out a leg, knocking him from his feet. The knife clattered to the floor, sliding across the smooth stone and resting at the statue's feet. Tumult's form wavered, slipping away, but I refused to continue his cowardly spar.

Clutching his arm, I sank my teeth into his flesh. Had I been in demon form, I could have bitten through bone. My blunt, human teeth lacked the strength to sink all the way through, so I bit hard and jerked my head, removing a chunk of his flesh.

I spat it into my hand and rose before kicking him in the gut. He groaned, his eyes growing wide with fear as he realized what I had done, and he scrambled to his feet, facing me in a defensive stance.

"What's wrong, my friend?" I asked, my tone

condescending. "Are you unable to hide without your body intact?"

His eyes narrowed, his glare turning to ice. "I will heal."

"Not while I still have breath in my lungs." I leaped toward the knife, sliding across the floor, my arm outstretched.

With Tumult in his demon form and I in my human, his speed surpassed mine fivefold. He kicked the knife, and it slid into a crevice beneath the statue's feet, leaving me weaponless against his talons and horns.

I stood and fisted my hands. "No one can take my place. I was created to stand by Lucifer's side, and to his side I will return."

"And what of your little witch? Even with your blood bond, spending too long in Hell will drive her mortal soul to madness." Tumult laughed. "Perhaps, if you could complete your quest...if you sacrificed her to our king...he might forgive your transgressions. But without Hecate..." He shrugged. "It's time for the Underworld to evolve, and for that, it needs new leadership."

I tightened my fists, my weak human nails digging into my palms. He made a point I hadn't considered. Cinder and I shared much more than a blood bond...a fact he was not privy to. Our soul bond would maintain her sanity, but she would never agree to abandon her family and stay by my side in Hell.

We would find Hecate. We would return her to Lucifer. But never would I sacrifice my witch to his whims. She would return home if I had to take her there myself...and then what?

Return to Hell, rule with Lucifer and my brothers as we had done for millennia? It was our duty. Our birthright.

Our burden.

Tumult tensed, ready to charge. But not at me. Instead, he turned on his heel and bolted for the wall I had created to keep Cinder safe. His horns hit the stone, cracking the magic I'd used to create it. He reared back and plowed into it again. It splintered. One more thrust and he would get through.

He turned toward me and sneered. "I've decided to kill your witch first, so you can watch her suffer."

His words lit a fire inside me unlike anything I'd ever felt. All logical thought slipped from my mind, leaving behind only pure, primal rage.

Hellfire coursed through my veins, a burst of magic from the core of my being healing every injury I had sustained. Power built in the nucleus of every cell in my body, bleeding outward until my skin hummed with energy, and the strength of twenty demons surged through my muscles.

"Cinder is mine," I growled, my demon boiling beneath the surface, demanding to be unleashed.

Tumult grinned wickedly. "Only if you can get to her first." He turned to the wall, taking a step back and coiling his muscles to strike.

Not even Lucifer could keep my rage contained.

I roared and charged, my demon clawing its way to the surface, breaking through the binding magic and unleashing its fury. I grabbed Tumult by the shoulders and hurled him across the room. He crashed into the wall, the force splintering the stone. Three massive cracks jutted up to the ceiling, and powdered stone rained onto the floor.

Tumult recovered, standing upright and running his finger over his healed arm. With his flesh reformed, he could now slip in and out of this plane. His form shimmered. I shot toward him, claws outstretched, and I swung, slicing off his finger.

He wailed, blood pouring from the wound. The injury tied him to this plane, but it didn't slow him down. He slammed his shoulder into my gut and lifted me, spinning in a circle before slinging me toward Hecate's statue. My back hit her raised torch, breaking it off at her hand. It tumbled to the ground, shattering as I hit the wall behind her and fell.

Tumult lowered his horns and barreled toward the failing magical wall. I scrambled to my feet and blocked him, landing an uppercut to his jaw that sent him careening into a support column. The impact knocked it loose. The base slid back while the upper part screeched across the ceiling, stopping at a thirty-degree angle.

"No woman is worth this much trouble." Tumult spat blood, and his claws protruded to their full extent.

I plowed toward him. He countered, and we met in the center of the room, flesh slamming into flesh, horns locking as we wrestled. I jerked my head and threw him aside. He hit the other dog statue, knocking it off its base and making the temple groan. More stone dust rained from above. Cracks jutted this way and that, spiraling up the columns and weakening the walls.

He roared, blowing smoke from his nostrils and striding toward me with his fists clenched. He punched. I ducked, feinting left before landing a fist in his face. He stumbled back, his eyes watering, and lashed out a claw, striking me in the stomach.

It was merely a flesh wound this time. I extended my claws and jabbed for his heart. He turned, and they sank into his side. He spun, lifting his leg, his foot hitting my chest. I flew backward, smacking into the statue's robes. Cracks crept up the goddess's form.

"I did not come here to destroy a temple." I grabbed Tumult by the neck and flung him against the wall. "But I will do whatever it takes to keep Cinder safe."

He grunted with the impact but landed on his feet. "And you're doing a stellar job thus far. I've seen how many times she's nearly died in your care."

His words struck a nerve, making my anger burn hotter. "You've seen nothing. You're a spineless imp who hides behind cowardly magic."

"Not hiding. Watching." He cracked his knuckles. "Calculating. Gauging your strength. Using you to take out the competition before I swooped in and claimed the prize."

"Relying on someone else to fight your battles, as usual. Pathetic."

"Perhaps I won't kill your witch. I believe I'll keep her as my slave." He charged, and I stepped out of the way, tripping him. He flailed, hitting the statue and cracking it more before he advanced once again.

As long as there was breath in my lungs, no one would lay a finger on my soulbride. Hellfire consumed all thought, rational or otherwise. My vision tunneled until all I could see was his chest. I barely noticed the sensation of his claws swiping across my face as I sank mine deep inside him and twisted them, shredding his heart.

His eyes bulged, and he wheezed, the light in them dimming to darkness. With one final thrust, I flung him across the room. His lifeless body landed in the crook of Hecate's elbow, the impact cracking her statue even more before he crumbled into dust... obliterated.

My breath came out in a rush, and my stomach churned with nausea. I doubled over, the adrenaline and power draining from my system as quickly as it had entered. Unable to hold on to my demonic form, my body morphed into human. I stumbled toward my clothes, but my demon had shredded them.

A loud crack echoed in the chamber. Hecate's statue split and crumbled, her head breaking into a hundred pieces as it hit the floor. The walls groaned. Slabs of stone fell from above. The angled column toppled.

"Cinder!" I rushed toward the magical wall. "Cinder, we must run."

CHAPTER 5

CINDER

"Discord!" I slapped my palm against the stone. "Let me out."

Muffled growls and the sounds of a struggle emanated through the wall. I ran my hands along the smooth surface, searching for a seam or a hidden release switch or spot where his magic didn't solidify...anything to get me into that room so we could take out Tumult together.

It was as if the doorway never existed.

"You and your damn walls." I rested both hands against it, straining to hear the commotion. "For someone whose powers are waning, you sure spent a lot of vim on a stupid barricade."

I blew a hard breath through my nose and turned toward the hall of mirrors. Lighting a fireball in my hand, I touched the flames to the vat of oil, hoping to illuminate the room, but it didn't ignite.

The crimson sigils on the mirror in the distance brightened, pulsing, and a faint blue light glowed from the center of the glass. The temple groaned like it had when I'd shattered a mirror, the cracking sound of millennia-old stone making my muscles tense.

How could I have let Tumult lead us into a trap? He was here, waiting for us the moment we arrived, but... how? I definitely sensed Hecate when I scried. Did the asshat have the ability to enter my mind? To manipulate my visions?

Or had he simply followed us here? With his ability to disappear, he could have been riding along with us the entire time, waiting for the most dramatic moment to make his appearance.

The mirror hummed, drawing me from my thoughts, and I moved toward it. My abdomen tightened, my mouth going dry as I cautiously put one foot in front of the other. If Tumult had set this all up, it could be another part of the trap. Maybe he materialized the mirrors like Discord could walls. He certainly didn't place them all one by one.

Or did he? Honestly, I had no clue what other powers he possessed.

The humming intensified, drawing me deeper into the room. I glanced into the first mirror, and my breath caught. I spun to face its twin and then turned back to the first one. The mirrors reflected each other, going on and on, into infinity, but I...

I still had no reflection at all.

Unease made my stomach sour, but I pushed on, pausing to look into the next one. I held up my firelight, stepping closer to the glass. Still, I had no reflection.

"What the hell?" I reached forward, tentatively pressing my fingertips to the glass, half-expecting them to pass right through. The surface was solid. I rested both palms against it and applied pressure. It didn't give.

It would be my luck if Tumult had shoved me into the ether, and now I hung in limbo, here but not really here. My sweaty handprints marred the glass, so I had to be on this plane.

"Why no reflection?"

The sigils on the mirror in the distance glowed brighter. The hum intensified. Goosebumps pricked my skin. This long, narrow room should have been filled with thousands of Cinders, reflections of me as I passed each mirror.

Instead, I was completely, utterly, painfully alone.

I took a deep breath, centering myself, the gravity of my predicament settling heavily on my shoulders. I had no idea what was happening in the other room. The only thing I knew for certain was that Discord was still alive. How long he'd remain in that state, I had no clue.

My pulse thrummed, and I extinguished my flame. I needed to look into the mirror that called to me. Whether Tumult set this up or not, there was only one way in and out of this chamber...and my dear, sweet demon had barricaded the door.

I was trapped, alone, and I really, *really* needed to pee.

My throat thickened, and I swallowed hard before stepping in front of the mirror. My breath came out in a rush as I took in my reflection. The mirror opposite mine didn't reflect my image back, though. I turned, looking into it, but it was as if I wasn't there.

I spun to the illuminated one. The sigils surrounding it pulsed softly, some of them familiar, others I had never seen. If only Ash were here. She could decipher whatever message someone had engraved in the glass. She was the smartest person I knew.

If Ember were here, Tumult wouldn't have stood a chance. She'd have skewered him the second he materialized in the room. I loved fighting alongside my sister. She was the fiercest woman I knew.

My chest tightened, a homesick feeling making it ache. The three of us together were an unstoppable force, but I... Dammit, I shouldn't have come here alone. Everything I had done for the past year went against my very nature.

The secrets, the lies, the solitary actions. I *hated* being alone.

I gazed at my reflection, at my disheveled hair and the dark circles beneath my eyes. My mom had been training me to be self-sufficient my entire life. *Being high priestess is a lonely undertaking,* she would say, *but it's a burden you must learn to bear on your own.*

But what did she know? My mom didn't have sisters. She didn't understand what it was like to be forced to keep secrets from the people she loved the most. And she wasn't truly alone as high priestess. She'd married my dad when she was eighteen, long before she ascended to the position. She had a partner, someone she confided in.

My sisters used to be my partners, but training to run the coven isolated me, forbade me from sharing things with them, and I hated it. I hated everything about it.

The humming intensified, the red sigils pulsing brighter, demanding my attention. In the center of the mirror, an elemental fire witch sigil glowed deep blue...exactly where I had drawn it in my breath.

I touched the glass, tracing my fingers over my sigil and then the others. Nothing happened, so I tried again, going the opposite direction. "I don't know what you want me to do."

The sound of something hard hitting stone echoed from the other end of the room. I jerked my head toward the sound, hoping to see Discord charging through, but the wall remained intact.

The mirror, with its glowing sigils, showed me nothing more than the lonely woman staring back at me. If this was some sort of test, I was failing miserably.

"I've got nothing." I shrugged and lit another fire-ball before pacing to the end of the room. Holding the flames toward the wall, I searched for another way out. This wall was as solid as the front.

I peered along the row of mirrors to my left and then to my right. They had all been placed flush with the wall, so unless one of them was a hidden doorway, there was no way in or out of this place without Discord's help.

Of course, I had to try them all.

I ran my fingers along the edges of the nearest mirror. I found no seam, no indentation, no bump to indicate where the mirror ended and the wall began. I tried the one across from it, but it felt the same. I worked my way down the wall, feeling, searching, hoping to no avail. The reflective glass was a part of the stone, no doubt magically created when the temple was erected.

I returned to the glowing mirror, the only one that

offered my reflection, and extinguished my flames. "Hecate, please hear my plea."

A loud crash sounded from the other room, like stone cracking against stone. The temple groaned again, and bits of basalt fell from the ceiling. Whatever the boys were up to out there, I needed to figure out this puzzle before the entire temple collapsed on top of me.

Okay, think, Cinder. This mirror, these sigils... I highly doubted this was the work of a demon. I recognized the strength sigil on the right side of the glass, and one for endurance was etched into the bottom left. They were witchcraft symbols. The mirrors seemed to be part of the temple, which meant whatever test this was, it came from the goddess.

Good. Witchcraft I could handle. A demonic trap, not so much.

"Show me what you need me to see." I stared through the fire symbol, letting my vision soften so I could hopefully receive whatever message Hecate had for me. My eyes watered at the brightness of the sigils, and as the light intensified, I had to squint. The symbols dimmed, and the rest of the room plunged into darkness. I mean, complete, utter, total darkness. Seriously, I couldn't see anything but my reflection... not even my hand in front of my face.

"Okay, I take it you want me to see myself." I laughed dryly. "Here I am. All alone."

My heart sank at my words. "I know. I need to get used to it. Is that what you want me to see? That my birthright, my duty to my coven, comes first and I need to prepare myself for a lonely life?"

I'd hoped my revelation would reignite the firelight, or a secret door would open behind me. Hell, I'd have settled for a ringing bell and a *winner, winner, chicken dinner*. Anything to say I'd passed the test and could find Hecate and end this nightmare. But nothing happened. My reflection didn't change. The same miserable woman, who looked like she hadn't slept in a week, stared back at me.

"I don't understand why it has to be this way." I shifted my weight to my right leg. "I get tradition. I get ritual. But sometimes, doing things a certain way because that's how they've always been done does more harm than good."

The crimson light pulsed twice, and I crossed my arms.

"Or is this because I broke the rules? Am I supposed to see that I shouldn't have told my sisters about the curse? That this was my burden to bear alone because every high priestess before me handled it on her own? If so, I call bullshit."

The fire sign wavered, the blue glow around it growing larger, egging me on.

"A coven should be able to operate in whatever manner works best. My sisters are as much a part of the Holland bloodline as I am. I should have brought them in on the secrets as soon as I learned them, because a true leader keeps her people informed."

The fire sigil flashed, its blinding light freezing me to the spot. I no longer saw myself reflected in the mirror. Instead, my mind floated in the ether, in a trance similar to scrying, though I wasn't searching for anyone but myself.

Or maybe I was.

Deep down, in the core of my being, I knew I needed my sisters. The vision showed me flashes of them in the earthly realm. Ash burning through roots, Ember slaying demons, both battling fae bigger than any I'd ever seen. The veil had grown so thin...and it kept getting thinner. They couldn't mend it on their own.

It would take all of us...all *six* of us...to make things right again.

I gasped, my vision returning to the mirror's reflection, only this time, Ash and Ember stood behind me. I whirled to face them, but of course they weren't there.

They needed me, though. They needed me to survive Lucifer's games and get the hell out of...well, to get the hell out of Hell.

"Hecate, please show me where you are." I turned back to the mirror and froze. Sharp pain sliced into my temple, like an ice pick slowly sinking into my brain. Flashes of images pierced the otherwise total darkness, but I couldn't make out anything.

The building shook. A loud crash sounded behind me, but my body wouldn't move. The flashes grew brighter, flickering faster as if someone were fanning the pages of a book.

"Slow down." I tensed, ignoring the stones falling around me and focusing only on the images the ether showed me. I reached with my mind, pushing through a gelatinous sludge and stopping the pages from turning. A path. A location. But Hecate wasn't there.

"Why show me…?" The location pulsed, demanding attention, emphasizing its importance before another, absolutely horrifying vision entered my mind.

Hecate bound in chains.

CHAPTER 6

DISCORD

"Cinder!" I pounded the sides of my fists against the wall as the temple crumbled around me. The magic flashed, wavering beneath what little strength I had left, yet the wall held. I pounded it again, slamming my shoulder against it three times, using more force with each succession.

What was left of Hecate's statue split vertically behind me. One side crashed toward the temple entrance, stones shattering on the portico and rolling down the steps, the thunderous sound deafening. The other half remained upright, teetering on its pedestal.

I slammed my shoulder against the wall once more, but still it would not yield.

"Cinder, step away from the doorway." I hoped to Hades she heard my command.

Dodging falling stones, I raced to the statue and braced my hands against the side, pushing with all my might. Sweat beaded on my forehead as I strained against its weight. I pressed my back against it, using my legs as leverage. It rocked. I pushed harder. More stone cracked. The statue fell, crashing into the wall and shredding the magical fibers I had created.

The ceiling buckled. A slab of stone the size of a tar pit plunged to the ground. I leaped over it and sprinted into the next room. Moonlight streamed in through the massive holes in the ceiling, and the walls groaned with the temple's shifting weight.

Cinder stood near the center of the long, narrow room, oblivious to the destruction around her. She stared into a mirror, her eyes glazed as if she were in a trance, her jaw slack, her lips parted.

"Cinder, we must leave." I paced toward her.

She didn't respond, didn't acknowledge my presence. A new fury boiled inside me. If Tumult had done something to her mind, I would... Damn it, I had already killed him, decimated his soul, so there wasn't much else I could do.

I should have let him live so I could kill him with newfound fury.

"Cinder." I stood behind her, clutching her shoulders and giving her a gentle shake. When she didn't react, I scooped her into my arms and powered through the ruins toward the exit, my leg muscles burning with the exertion.

Cinder gasped, jerking her head up. "Wait! I wasn't done."

"The temple is done with us." I leaped over a crumbled column, rolling my ankle as I hit the floor, my foot slicing open on a shard of obsidian.

Pain shot up my leg, making me bite my tongue, but still I plowed ahead. I made it to the portico and barreled down the steps as the columns supporting the pediment fell toward each other with a thunderous boom.

I ran halfway up the walk before lowering Cinder's feet to the ground and turning to witness the rest of the destruction. What was left of the temple collapsed inward on itself, stone crumbling and obsidian shattering until only a pile of rubble remained.

Cinder raised her fingers to her lips. "Oh, my goddess, Discord. What did you do?"

I cared not for the accusation in her tone. "I saved your life and mine."

"By destroying Hecate's temple?" Her mouth hung agape.

"Had I not, we would both be dead." I lowered onto a large stone and rested my ankle on my knee to examine the shard of obsidian embedded in the arch of my foot. I yanked out the offending object, and blood spurted from the wound.

Cinder snapped her mouth shut, finally coming to her full senses. "Ouch. Looks like you hit an artery."

"Whatever makes you say that?" I squeezed the sides of the wound, holding them together to speed my healing. When I let go, more blood spouted, as if I'd created a fountain of my foot.

"Wait... Why are you naked?" She furrowed her brow and kneeled in front of me, opening her backpack and retrieving a strip of fabric before wrapping it tightly around my arch.

"Is that your underwear?" I asked.

"You never know when you'll need to change your skivvies, so I bought extra." She tied the ends in a knot and rose, wiping her hands on her pants and wincing.

"You expect me to wear your panties on my foot?"

"Well, they're definitely too small to hold your junk. And speaking of your junk..." She glanced at the clotted blood on her palm before arching a brow at me. "Why are you naked?"

"My demon form is much larger than this one. When I transformed, it shredded my clothes." I adjusted the fabric, tightening the knot.

Her face pinched in an adorably confused way. "I thought you couldn't shapeshift anymore."

"It appears that our bond...my feelings for you... allowed me to push through Lucifer's bind to save your life. Tumult is no more."

Her lips parted again, surprise lifting her brows. "You... To save...? You have all your powers back?"

"Unfortunately, no." I rose and tested my weight on my injured foot. "If that were the case, I would have healed by now and we'd be well on our way to our next destination. Did you locate Hecate?"

"I was about to, but you yanked me out of the trance." Her gaze bounced to my dick three times before she looked into my eyes.

"Would you prefer that I had not?" I gestured to the rubble and willed my soldier to remain at ease, which was no easy feat. A bead of sweat dripped down her forehead, giving me the sudden urge to lick her from head to toe.

Yes, the timing was inappropriate, yet the urge remained.

"I suppose not." She bit her bottom lip, her gaze dancing around my face as if she, too, were fighting the attraction. "Thank you."

"You're welcome," I said, shifting my weight to the uninjured foot. "How is your hand?"

"It's just a little cut, I'll be fine." Sympathy softened her eyes. "Can you walk?"

"Of course." The excruciating pain shooting up my leg begged to differ, but I would not show weakness in front of this woman.

"Come on then." She jerked her head toward the end of the path. "Hecate has a safehouse, kinda like your secret hideout. We can go there to regroup and hopefully find you some clothes."

"You communicated with the goddess?" Surprise lifted my brows, and I walked next to her, the stabbing pain in my foot slowly easing to a steady burn.

"Sorta." She turned left at the end of the path and started toward the back of the temple. "She's incapacitated, but she managed to send me a little information."

"Incapacitated how?"

She frowned and shook her head. "I need a minute to sort it all out. It was confusing."

My foot landed on a jagged rock, and I fought a groan. "Where is the safehouse located?"

"I'm not sure." She turned her head slightly, as if to look at me, but jerked her gaze forward again.

"Then why are we walking in this direction?"

She lifted her hands and dropped them at her sides. "I'm just following the pull."

We continued on, she following the pull, I following her, until we reached the cave at the end of the valley. My foot was healing, albeit much more slowly than I liked, but the intense fatigue weighing my body down was nearly unbearable. I needed to press her, to insist she explain in great detail every-thing she saw while in the trance, so we could devise a plan.

But at the moment, I was too tired to care.

Cinder paused and turned to me. "Have you been inside there before?"

"I have not." I rested a hand against the mouth of the cave, using the rock to support my weight. "I never knew it was here until today."

She raised an arm toward me. The fine hairs stood on end along her goosebumped skin. "There's a lot of magic inside. If I had a spell kit, I could figure out what kind. Do you sense anything negative?"

My elbow buckled, and my shoulder slammed against the wall. Nausea churned in my gut, and an intense, dull pain formed in my right temple. "I sense myself blacking out soon if I don't find a place to lie down."

Concern creased her brow, and she clutched my arm with both hands, pulling me to her side. "Inside we go then. Come on."

I stumbled forward. Cinder steadied me with a hand on my chest before placing my arm across her shoulders and sidling next to me, absorbing my weight.

Heat crept up my neck, a hollow pit forming in my stomach. What had become of the first Prince of Hell?

I wore a woman's panties on my injured foot. Using magic I was born with had fatigued me beyond measure, and now my soulbride, strong as she was, struggled beneath my weight. I should have been the one carrying her. Never in my existence had I felt this weak...this defeated. I tried to pull from her grasp, but she held me tightly.

"Let me help you," she said softly.

My face flushed, heat spreading across my cheeks and making my ears burn, my embarrassment refusing to allow her coddling. "I don't need help. I am a Prince of Hell. I..."

"*You* are an injured demon." She wrapped her arms around me. "And *we* are a team. Don't make me scoop you up and cradle you like a baby."

She stepped forward, pulling me with her. I wanted to protest more, but buzzing energy engulfed us the moment we entered the cave. A flash of soothing blue light filled the space, making stars dance in my vision, and a coolness washed over me, the scents of lilac and cinnamon replacing the sulfurous stench of the valley.

Cinder gasped, a sense of wonder filling her voice as she uttered, "Holy Hecate. Are you seeing this?"

"I..." The blue light tunneled. Searing pain seized my muscles. I saw nothing.

CHAPTER 7

CINDER

Magic sparkled all around us, like silver stars against a midnight blue sky. It swirled and spun, dancing this way and that, a display of intricate choreography set to a silent song. Cool air caressed my skin for the first time since I arrived in Hell, and warm floral notes, laced with cinnamon, tamed the stench of Underworld funk.

The silver sparkles parted, creating a tunnel in front of us, and a trail of glitter spiraled down the path, beckoning me forward. My legs started to move of their own volition, my body accepting the invitation without a thought from my mind, but I paused.

It was time for a serious vibe check, because who knew what lay deep inside this cave. "Do you sense anything?"

I turned to Discord, but his eyes had glazed. His jaw hung slack, and his shallow breaths seemed labored. Blood soaked the undies tied to his foot, and a massive bruise marred the left side of his stomach.

Good vibes or bad, standing here wasn't helping him in the slightest. I sidled closer, wrapping my arms around him and coaxing him forward, into the magical tunnel. Hecate wouldn't steer a faithful witch wrong... I hoped.

On we went, following the spiral of magic. The air felt light and crisp, and it energized my body, replacing my fatigue with newfound hope. Yes, someone was holding the goddess hostage somewhere in the Underworld, which was a very bad thing. But she had communicated with me. Her messages had arrived in bits and pieces, a puzzle I couldn't wait to solve.

First, though... I had to take care of the big, sexy oaf leaning on my shoulder.

I had a feeling demons weren't meant to venture through this tunnel, and much like how Discord's space-bendy magic drained me, Hecate's goddess-level witchcraft affected him in a not-so-nice way.

But you should never ignore your instincts, and my gut said the only way out was through. I turned around to confirm my suspicion, and sure enough, the mouth of the cave had closed behind us.

The sparkling tunnel seemed to stretch into

infinity before us, but after only five more steps, a wavering wall of blue-green magic appeared, blocking the path.

"The only way out is through," I repeated my instinct's mantra and dragged my demon into the portal. I passed the threshold easily, but getting Discord through was like pulling a two-hundred-pound bag of rocks through a massive gelatin mold.

I strained, forcing his body through until a loud popping sound nearly busted my eardrums. The air pressure shifted, lightening first, taking the breath from my lungs before the heavy, sulfurous atmosphere of the Underworld pressed in around me.

"I did not miss this smell." I wrinkled my nose.

Discord sucked in a sharp breath. His knees buckled, but I managed to keep him upright.

"Are you okay?" I asked.

"Never better," he rasped.

"Liar." We stood just inside the tunnel exit, on the edge of yet another town.

In the distance, scary-ass demons skulked about, walking the streets and going in and out of shops. The buildings looked like they used to be nice, but after centuries of neglect, they'd fallen into disrepair. Potholes dotted the streets, and a brawl—from what I could only imagine was a bar—spilled out onto the sidewalk.

"We're back in the eighth level, aren't we?" I asked.

"Indeed, and in the seediest village imaginable." He winced as he took a step. "Do you sense the safehouse?"

I closed my eyes and took a deep breath, focusing on the image Hecate had shown me at the temple. A tingle formed beneath my breastbone, a magical tug guiding me toward my destination. Was this what my dad felt when he used his location magic? If so, it was nothing short of amazing.

"Quickly." His left knee buckled, and I held him tighter.

"I found it, but there's a problem." I repositioned him, pushing my shoulder into his armpit to absorb his weight. "We can't parade you down the street naked and bloody."

"In this town, it won't matter. The inhabitants have seen much worse."

I didn't want to know the details. "Okay, but they'll recognize us, won't they? You, at the very least."

"Disguise us then." He squeezed his eyes shut. "Bloody our faces or leave me here. I'm fading."

"Bloody our...?" I glanced around the tunnel. The magic had dissipated, and we now stood at the very mundane mouth of the cave. Or...if we had entered through the mouth near Hecate's temple, did that make this the ass?

It didn't matter. There had to be some mud or dirt

around that we could smear on our faces. Anything but blood. Sadly, only solid rock surrounded us.

"Cinder..." His lids fluttered, his eyes rolling back.

"Crap. I'm on it." I grabbed my last knife, contemplating where to cut. His blood on him, mine on me. Who knew how long it would take him to heal, though? And with my pain tolerance at a negative ten, cutting myself wasn't the slightest bit appealing either.

I scooted him to the right, leaning him against the cave wall. "Do not fall down. I'm not sure I can get you back up if you do."

He only grunted in reply. Keeping one hand on his body to hold him against the wall, I slowly bent until I reached the undies on his foot. The blood had stopped gushing, thankfully, and as I untied the makeshift bandage, only a few drops oozed from the wound.

His knees bent, and he slumped downward. I shot to my feet and grabbed him around the chest before he could tumble, situating my shoulder against his armpit once more.

Never did I ever think I would need to smear bloody panties over someone's face—especially my own—yet here we were. The fabric dripped like Aunt Flo had spilled a week's worth of tomato juice all at once, and I curled my lip as my stomach turned.

Discord wheezed, spurring me into action. I

rubbed the bloody undies over his face, dabbing a little extra around his eyes while leaving a few spots of bare skin to break up his features.

Next up...me. I smeared the blood on like Viking warpaint and shoved the panties into my pocket. *So gross.*

"Here we go." Tightening my grip on my demon, I guided him out of the cave and into the city.

Very few people here had human forms. Most looked like monsters, with flat noses, bull horns, and muscular, top-heavy builds. Some had hooves, while others sported taloned toes, and they all reeked of sweat, stale booze, and sulfur.

Music blasted from a bar, the bass so loud and low it could have altered my heartbeat if I stuck around long enough. And that brawl on the sidewalk...? Good goddess, these guys were vicious.

Punches cracked bones, and claws split skin. I tried to give it a wide berth as I dragged Discord toward the safehouse, but a particularly beefy fellow tossed a tall, lanky demon toward me as if the guy were made of straw. The demon landed at my feet, and I furrowed my brow, doing my best not to allow my reaction to match my emotions.

I wanted to run, to get the hell off this street and into the safety of Hecate's sanctuary, but we'd never make it there alive if they suspected who we were. I had to act like a demon.

"Watch it," I growled, though I sounded more like a fluffy kitten than the bear I tried to emulate.

The beefy guy roared and leaped, landing on top of Mr. Lanky and clutching the back of his neck.

"Don't look," Discord wheezed, so you know I absolutely had to.

Mr. Beefy extended his thick claws, sinking them into Lanky's neck and wrapping them around his vertebrae. With a guttural roar, he yanked his arm back, ripping the guy's spine from his body—*Mortal Kombat* style.

My stomach lurched, but instead of tossing my cookies into the street, I glowered and kept walking.

"Who are you?" Beefy called behind me.

"Mind your business. I'm hungry," I said, making my voice as deep and gruff as it would go. We hung a left at the corner, and thank the goddess, Hecate's house lay four yards ahead. At least, the magical tug that had guided me here claimed it was her house.

I couldn't tell you what I expected to find. The vision she'd shown me had been hazy at best, more of a feeling...or knowing...than a visual image. This run-down shack with peeling paint, broken steps, and shattered windows definitely wasn't it. Thorny brambles crawled up the walls, and fissures jutted in different directions all around the yard.

Discord stumbled beside me as we approached. He made it up the first step when he gasped, his eyes going wide before rolling back until only the whites remained. He collapsed, pitching forward onto the porch and taking me down with him.

My shoulder hit the stone, sharp pain exploding down my arm, and I groaned. Discord lay motionless, his upper body face-down on the porch, the rest of him dangling down the steps, bare butt up, mooning the orange moon.

I pushed to sitting, rubbing my shoulder as six demons approached the house. My pulse sprinting, I scrambled to my feet and reached for my knife, but the beasties stopped, turned in circles, and scratched their heads as if we were invisible. One of them pointed to the right, the others nodded, and they strode away.

Huh. How about that? Maybe we *were* invisible here. That would sure be a welcome relief. I turned and reached for the doorknob, but it unlatched and swung open before I could touch it.

"Please tell me this place isn't haunted," I muttered. Although...since I was a dead witch and he was a demon, I supposed we'd be the ones doing the haunting.

Now, how to get a two-hundred-pound, unconscious man across the threshold? I started to grab his wrists and pull, but he was naked and face down. I doubted he'd appreciate his man bits scraping across the rough stone porch, so that idea was out.

I kneeled beside him, resting a hand on his shoulder. "Discord? If you've got any energy left at all, now would be the time to get up and at least crawl through the door."

A bit of drool rolled from the corner of his mouth. Lovely.

Squatting, I braced the heel of one hand against his shoulder, the other against his hip, and shoved, using my legs as leverage and rolling him to his back. His dangly bits flopped, drawing my gaze, which was totally inappropriate in a situation like this. I needed to get him inside and comfortable before I gawked at the sheer perfection that was Discord.

"Here we go." I hooked my arms beneath his pits and gritted my teeth, straining as I dragged him into the foyer. Once I got his feet inside and out of the way, I kicked the door shut, turning to take in the rat-infested disaster of a shack.

Only, there wasn't a rat in sight, and the disaster...? I rubbed my eyes. This couldn't be the same run-down hovel I'd entered.

A polished obsidian floor reflected the moonlight streaming in through the *not-broken* windows, and deep-blue protection sigils glowed on the gray slate walls. The air felt cool by Underworld standards, and the scents of lilacs and cinnamon provided a welcome relief from the rotten egg scent I would never get accustomed to.

A living room lay to my left, complete with a plush,

midnight rug and an antique sofa with dark purple upholstery and carved cherry wood. A short hallway extended back from the living room, and I glimpsed an herb-stocked kitchen through an arched doorway to my right. My stomach growled on cue.

I dragged Discord into the living room, getting as much of his body onto the rug as I could. There was no way I could get him onto the couch, much less into a bed, so this would have to do. His chest rose and fell rhythmically, his eyes moving back and forth behind his lids. The gash on his foot was nearly healed, but unless the obsidian he'd cut it on was laced with poison, I doubted that was the reason for his current state.

He had transformed into his demon. He'd dug deep into his soul and given Lucifer's power-stripping hold a giant middle finger. Sure, he was paying the price now, but he had beaten the devil himself, even if for only a few minutes.

And he'd done it for *me*. Cue the warm fuzzies.

To say I was in awe of this man would be an understatement. He was complex. Broody and lethal, full of rage, yet tender when he wanted to be.

Get yourself together, girl. You are not falling for a demon. If only I could convince myself.

I ducked down the hall and found a bedroom, complete with a king-sized bed, a dresser, and an ornate armoire with lilies and the triple moon symbol embossed in the wood. Inside the armoire, I found a pillow and a blanket, so I grabbed them and headed back to my demon.

Once I got Discord snug as a bug, I headed to the kitchen. A massive wood-burning stove stood in the far corner, and bundles of dry herbs hung from a cord stretched across the ceiling. It felt weird AF rummaging through the goddess's cabinets, but I had to do it. She wouldn't have shown me this place if she didn't want me to use it, right?

Goddess, I hoped not. We'd already destroyed her temple. I could only imagine how pissed she'd be about that.

First things first. We needed food. I opened cabinet after cabinet, high ones and low ones, but I couldn't find a single edible morsel. Unless we wanted to munch on a salad of dried herbs, we were out of luck in the meal department. Damn.

I plopped onto a stool and set my backpack on the counter to rummage through it. Granola bar wrappers, an empty water bottle, a candle, and a few jars of who-knew-what herbs. If the seer were still alive, I'd get her a label maker for Yule. I found ten ashmarks in the front pocket, but that wouldn't get me much.

I set the candle in front of me and shot a stream of fire toward the wick. As the flame flickered, I softened my gaze, allowing it to blur, and pressed my palms together. "Thank you, Hecate, for offering your home to us. I'm sorry about the temple, but if you'll continue guiding us, I will find a way to make it up to you."

I took a deep breath, feeling, listening, searching for a sign that she heard me.

My stomach growled again, and I closed my eyes for a long blink, loath to do what I had to do next.

CHAPTER 8
CINDER

Discord lay sleeping on the floor as I slipped out the front door and made my way back into the city. The corpse of the spineless demon still lay in the street near the bar, so I turned in the opposite direction and headed for what I hoped was a quieter part of town.

Hope...

My entire existence, the fate of my coven, of Salem, hell...maybe of the world...all hinged on that one little word. My sisters had done well so far. Ash had found my journal, they'd summoned Chaos and Mayhem, and they'd tried to call Discord. He'd be there now, ending the curse and mending the veil if not for this little snafu.

If I'd known about the amulet, that I'd be stuck here for eternity without it, I might have rethought this adventure. Or not. I honestly thought I'd be in and out quickly, that my sisters never would've needed to get involved.

Some High Priestess I'd turned out to be, clinging to the hope that my sisters were accomplishing the task that belonged to me. The hope that I would find my parents, find Hecate, make it out of Hell alive...

Right now, though, the only hope I needed to focus on was that I would find food and supplies and make it back to the safehouse without battling a dozen beasties who had every reason to challenge me.

Because I was about to rob them blind.

I walked two blocks without incident, thankfully. The demons hanging around outside the shops stared. A few whispered as I passed, but with my face covered in blood, my clothes torn, and my hair in knots, I blended in with the riffraff fairly well.

At the end of the third block, I found a massive warehouse-type building with obsidian doors and a glowing sign written in demonic sigils. I *hoped* it was a welcome sign. Apparently, hope was my brand now.

Straightening my spine and lifting my chin, I strolled inside like I owned the place. Two cashiers stood stationed at the checkout, the lines of customers stretching ten deep, while a dozen other registers sat empty. Whiny country music droned from the speakers above, and my boots stuck to the dirty floor, making a squishy sound with each step I took.

"Welcome to Hell," I muttered as I paced deeper into the store.

I should've been used to the "normalness" of the Underworld by now, but I couldn't help shaking my head as I passed rows and rows of metal shelving units, filled to the brim with everything a demon could need. They had cooking utensils, bath towels, beastie hygiene products, and even board games.

Black signs with glowing sigils marked what I assumed were the prices, and a demon wearing nothing but leggings and pasties on her six breasts handed out samples of some goddess-knew-what-kind of cereal.

I was famished, so I accepted what she offered. She poured a bit of milk into the tiny bowl, and I tipped my head back, dumping it into my mouth. It tasted salty, sweet, and slightly pungent, but the milk cut the bitterness, making it completely palatable.

I paused, my brow furrowing. What kind of animals did they milk in Hell? My gaze slid over the stickers on the woman's array of areolas, and I cringed. *Please don't tell me I just consumed demon breastmilk.*

I kept walking, lest my thoughts spiraled and my stomach lurched. I refused to even think about it. *Shudder.*

A burly guy with purple-gray scales stood behind a counter in the butcher section. He wielded a massive cleaver, slamming it onto the carcass of some poor beast, breaking the joints. The sound of bones cracking made my muscles crawl beneath my skin, so I focused on the clothing section ahead and picked up my pace.

Racks and shelves overflowed with garments in shades of black, red, and blacker black. I rummaged through their offerings, finding pants and shirts for all kinds of beasties. For humans? Not so much. I found jeans with four legs, huge sizes that could've accommodated three of me, and shirts with the armholes at the waist. The next rack, and the next one, offered much of the same.

I suppose that made sense in this town. The lower-level demons outnumbered the ones with a human form twenty to one. But there were humanoid beasties here, so there had to be something that would fit. I made my way to the back of the store and found two lonely racks with normal clothes. Well, normal to me, anyway.

I grabbed us both three outfits, some socks, undies, and a pair of boots for Discord since he'd shredded his, and I shoved them into a big leather bag before heading back to the grocery section. I loaded the bag with stinky bottled water, granola bars, dried meat, and anything else I could find that didn't require cooking.

With my supplies gathered, I chewed the inside of my cheek and eyed the checkout line. The ten ashmarks in my pocket wouldn't begin to cover everything we needed, so there was only one thing to do. I had to steal it.

My stomach soured at the thought. Light witches did not steal. It went against our moral code, against the very fiber of our beings. Our magic was a gift, and we only used it for good.

But what other choice did I have? Seriously, if someone wanted to offer another solution to this mess, I'd be all ears. Anyone...? No?

I shuffled forward, joining the line and considering my options. I could wait here, let the cashier ring me up, and then hope to Hecate I could convince him not to charge me. But that would take time. Plus, I'd have to convince the demon in line behind me as well, and that would take more vim than I could spare.

I would just have to make a run for it.

"Go ahead. I forgot something." I stepped out of line and gestured for the woman behind me to move forward. She curled her lip, giving me a once-over before filling in the gap.

I paced toward the exit and stopped at a display of canned mystery meat, pretending to examine it while I figured out my escape plan. A heavy hand landed on my shoulder, making my heart rocket into my throat, and I grabbed my knife before spinning toward the culprit.

"Where's your friend?" the spine ripper from the bar asked, his voice dripping with disdain.

"I ate him...like a mantis. You'd better pray I don't eat you too." I turned on my heel and strode for the exit, but a freaking centaur blocked my path. The half-man half-horse had black fur on his animal side, and he wore a leather scabbard on his back, the straps crisscrossing over his scarred, muscular chest.

"You gotta pay for that." He stomped a hoof and crossed his human arms. "Back in line."

"No. No, I really don't." I laid my magic on thick. "I don't have any money, and I need these supplies to save the realm. It's better if you let me pass so I can do my job and you can sleep soundly at night."

He lowered his brow, considering my words. "What do you mean 'save the realm'?"

"Those damn witches on the other side started summoning demons, and they tore apart the veil. If I don't fix it soon, Hell will implode. You don't want that on your conscience, do you?" I sent another pulse of magic toward him.

At least, I tried to.

The centaur screwed his mouth over to one side and looked at me like I'd grown six sets of ears. "Back in line or face the consequences." He flexed his biceps for emphasis.

"You want to let me pass," I tried again. "I'm your Obe-Wan Kenobi. Your only hope."

"There's no hope here." He reached behind his back and pulled out a crossbow, aiming it at my heart.

Another. Frigging. Crossbow. I had no intention of finding out if his arrows were poison-tipped.

Reaching deep into the core of my being, I called on my fire. My insides heated, and a surge of power coursed through my veins. I fisted my hand before uncurling my fingers and gathering a fireball in my palm. I could feel the crowd forming behind me, the low vibration palpable as they gathered to watch me square off with the centaur.

It looked like I'd be giving them a show. I hurled the ball o' flames at the beastie's chest, expecting it to at least burn through his scabbard straps and hurt like hell. But the moment it impacted his chest, it sputtered out like a birthday candle after a wish.

"What the eff?" I shook my hand and called on my fire again. My fingertips sparked, and a tiny flame ignited in my palm.

The centaur laughed and rested his finger on the trigger. "Is that all you've got?"

Apparently, it was, but I didn't have time to ponder my misfiring magic. Instead, I threw my knife. It circled pommel over tip, heading straight for his chest, but the bastard grabbed it by the blade and threw it to the ground. Blood poured from his palm, and he glowered, returning his crossbow to the scabbard before cracking his knuckles and stomping his hooves.

Oh, he wanted to fight hand to hand, did he? Well,

that seemed unfair. I could barely reach his horsy shoulder on my tippy toes.

Tightening my grip on my soon-to-be-stolen bag, I took two steps backward, but the horde behind me wasn't having it. Someone gripped my shoulders, and two sets of hands slammed into my back, shoving me toward the centaur. They closed in around us, creating a ring and shouting something about blood and tearing off body parts. I barely heard them over the sound of my pulse whooshing in my ears.

My boots stuck to the dirty floor as I shifted from foot to foot. The centaur reared back, his front hooves kicking at the air, his nostrils flaring with a snort. The crowd pressed closer, moving us farther from the exit, the air thick with the scents of sulfur and sweat.

My body tensed, instincts screaming at me to run, but the circle of spectators would never let me through. The exit stood unguarded behind the centaur, my only hope of escape...but I'd have to make it past him first.

He advanced, his muscles rippling beneath his fur, a wicked grin exposing teeth too sharp to be horse or human. I slipped my hand into the bag, searching for the set of steak knives I'd snagged from the kitchen section. My fingers found the box, but it was sealed with superglue.

The centaur lunged, hooves striking sparks on the stone floor as he came for me. I ducked beneath his swinging fist—which was no easy feat considering the span of his arms was double my height—and I darted left, crouching near the edge of our boxing ring.

"Fight, little girl. Entertain them." He snorted and feinted, his tail lashing in annoyance. "Draw first blood, and I might let you live."

Little girl…? Oh, no, he didn't.

"Don't you mean second blood? You're already acquainted with my knife." My fingers closed around something hard, and I yanked it from my bag and hurled it at him. A can of chili smacked him in the forehead, and he stumbled, grunting and shaking his head.

A ripple of laughter snaked through the crowd, their jeers briefly transforming into surprised cackles. The centaur staggered, his eyes burning with rage and confusion. Clearly, he hadn't expected his evening to include a food fight, yet there we were…and I was not above adding a little culinary humiliation to the menu.

I flung my elbow back, slamming it into a demon's nose. The guy faltered just enough for me to reach behind him and grab the mystery meat display and yank it forward. The shelving unit toppled, cans crashing to the ground and rolling in every direction.

I swiped two and chucked them both at the centaur. One got him in the stomach, making his human half double over. The other hit his horsy knee with a *thwack*. He snorted and stamped his hoof, lowering his torso and charging at me.

A hoof landed on a can, his weight smashing it open, spilling mystery meat all over the floor. His front leg slipped out from under him, and he crashed forward, his horse chest smacking the ground before he caught himself on his hands.

The crowd cheered, hooting and hollering as he tried to get his legs back under him, his hooves skittering wildly on a slick mosaic of mushy meat and sauce. I seized the moment, adrenaline surging through my veins, and dove for my fallen knife. My fingers grazed cold steel just as the centaur pounded a fist into the floor, sending cracks spiderwebbing through the stone.

He lunged for me, but his back legs fishtailed on a rogue can, his momentum throwing him off-balance again. I sprang to my feet, knife brandished, and faced him head-on as he scrambled to his hooves. The jeers from the crowd faded into a hush, tension crackling in the air like static before a storm.

The centaur reached behind his back, going for the crossbow, and that was my cue to ride like the wind. Muscles coiled, I pounded pavement toward him. He lowered the bow. His finger moved toward the trigger. I screamed like a banshee.

My boot hit a patch of wet meat, and I slipped,

slamming the knife into his horse chest before sliding beneath him like I was headed for home base. The doors whooshed open, and I shot to my feet, clutching the bag and what was left of the supplies as I plowed toward the safehouse.

The centaur roared from somewhere behind me, but I didn't dare turn around. Footfalls echoed, hooves and shoes, the sound of at least a dozen pursuers chasing me making my adrenaline spike again.

I darted around the corner half a second before an arrow whizzed past, and I laid on the speed, sprinting toward Hecate's shack and hurtling onto the porch. The mob following me ran straight past the house as if it were invisible, and I dragged in a massive breath, clutching the doorjamb and willing my heart to slow the eff down.

The door swung open, and I stumbled into the foyer before closing it and leaning my back against it. Pressing a hand to my chest, I closed my eyes and took three deep breaths, begging my heart to slow its pace before it exploded.

Battling a centaur security guard was definitely not on my bingo card today.

Neither was misfiring magic. I slipped the bag off my shoulder and held my hand up, trying to call a flame to life. All I managed were a couple of sparks.

This was not good. So very not good.

Fire was my inborn gift, my element. It was as much a part of me as the blood running through my veins, so how in all the realms could I not access it? Did Lucifer strip my powers too? Could he even do that?

I picked up the bag and headed to the living room to wake up Discord and get some answers...but he was gone.

"Discord?" I shouted, but he didn't respond. "I swear to Hecate, if you went off on your own..."

I strode through the living room and down the hall. The scents of patchouli and sandalwood drifted on the air, and as I entered the bedroom, I found my demon, freshly showered and sexy AF, sleeping beneath the sheets.

The perturbed sensation tightening my chest loosened, and I put the bag down, gently removing the contents and setting them on the dresser.

He looked so peaceful, serene almost, but far from harmless. Even dead to the world, his aura screamed danger and excitement. He lay on his side, his right hand beneath the pillow, his ribcage expanding and contracting with his breaths, and I had to admit my heart melted a little bit.

How my body found the time to feel attraction, kinship...anything at all...toward this man I had no clue. The hunters were still hunting, I'd royally pissed off a centaur three times my size, and we still didn't know where Hecate was. The apparent invisibility spell on this house was our only reprieve, and thank the goddess for it.

Twelve hours of deep sleep would do me good, but I'd settle for a shower and a cat nap. Based on what I'd felt when my sisters had tried to summon Discord, time moved faster in the earthly realm. Halloween was fast approaching, and while I'd have loved to take a break and chill here for a few days, I had a coven to save and a veil to mend.

I set a stack of Discord's clothes on the nightstand before heading to the bathroom and closing the door. Good goddess, I was a mess. I barely recognized the woman staring back at me in the mirror, but her bloody face and ratted hair weren't the problem.

Once full of vigor and vim, my eyes now appeared hollow, distant. I was losing myself in this realm, the constant flux between fight and flight taking a toll on my body and my mind. Hell was no place for the living.

I turned from the mirror and stepped into the shower, the scalding water pelting my face, rivulets of pink cascading down my body and spiraling into the drain. I washed my hair and scrubbed, standing beneath the stream until the water ran clear.

After drying off, I threw on some undies and a t-shirt—I'd deal with pants after my nap—and worked the tangles out of my hair with a wide-toothed comb. Steam wafted out as I opened the door, and I padded to the bed, slipping beneath the sheets and lying on my side, facing my demon.

CHAPTER 9

DISCORD

I kept my eyes closed as Cinder climbed into the bed with me. I was unready to face her expression of disdain, which she surely felt toward me after my display of weakness. She would never look at me the same again.

My body had healed with my slumber, but no remedy could mend my wounded pride.

I lay still and listened to the subtle shifts in the house—the pipes groaning, the hush of magic woven thick through the walls. My pulse thudded in my ears, each beat of my heart a metronome for regret. I had failed her, yet again, my body betraying me, rendering me incapable of carrying her through another nightmare.

Behind my eyelids, shadows flickered: memories of chaos, of blood and trembling hands, of magic denied.

I hadn't asked for redemption, but there it was, in the gentle way she'd set my clothes out, in the hope that trembled faintly beneath her exhaustion.

I could sense her, close now, her breath measured, her presence both a balm and a blade. The silence between us was heavy, punctured only by her soft snores and the distant thrum of the world outside. The temptation to reach for her, to seek solace in her embrace, warred against my shame, and I let the battle rage in the darkness of my mind.

She deserved so much more than I could provide her. Without my powers intact, I was as useless as an imp. Newfound anger ignited in my chest, and I focused on the burn. Cinder was meant to be my soul-bride. Of that I had no doubt, but the events that had led us to this union filled me with rage. Lucifer had no right to strip my powers, and Isabel... Once Cinder was safe at home, I would find the insolent witch's soul and torture her for eternity.

Another pang of regret expanded in my chest. Safe at home was where Cinder belonged. *Her* home. Not mine, for Hell was no place for the living. Ensuring her safe return had become my only priority, yet I longed to keep her here, by my side.

She snorted on a quick intake of breath, her hand absently swatting at her nose. I lifted the sheet, pulling it higher on her shoulder, and she stirred. Her lids fluttered, and I stilled my breathing as she snuggled into me, wrapping her arm around me and burying her face in my chest.

Her skin was warm and soft, a comfort that set my nerves on edge—a reminder that, while all was not yet lost, prevailing meant losing her, and *that* I would never survive.

A tremor passed through me, and I let my fingers edge closer to her shoulder. I stopped, just shy of contact, afraid the smallest touch would shatter the fragile calm we'd constructed. Afraid she would feel pity for me, disdain, or worse...nothing at all. The nightmare we were enduring tethered us, stitching our fates with threads of blood and longing, and I wondered now if she dreamed of escape.

Somewhere in the distance, a bell tolled, muffled by layers of stone and enchantment. The sound tugged at some primal part of me, a warning or perhaps an invitation. I forced myself to breathe, to anchor in the present, to resist the urge to flee back into sleep's oblivion.

Cinder tightened her embrace, and I rested my hand atop her shoulder as she whispered my name— not with accusation or pity, but with quiet certainty. The syllables curled in the air between us, tentative, raw, making the core of my being ache with need.

But bitterness simmered just beneath my skin. I would not forget what was taken from me. And as Cinder's eyes fluttered open, soft and luminous in the dim light, I made a silent vow: the reckoning would come. For now, though, I clung to the smallest mercy —a moment of peace in the bed we shared, deep in the heart of Hell.

A soft smile played on her features as she pulled her head back, her gaze flowing from my eyes to my mouth. She moistened her lips, the quick dart of pink slipping between them making blood rush to my groin.

She blinked, sucking in a quick breath as she awakened fully. "Oh, I'm sorry. I didn't mean to..." She started to pull away, but I tugged her closer.

"Don't apologize." I slid my hand to her face, brushing my thumb over her cheek. "It's an honor that you still take comfort in my embrace."

"An honor, huh?" She laughed. "You're a strong, sexy demon, who just saved my life. Why wouldn't I?"

I frowned. "Because of the multiple times you have had to save mine."

Her brow furrowed as if my words confused her. "We're a team. Of course, we look out for each other."

"I am not accustomed to showing weakness." I rolled to my back and dragged my hands down my face, humiliation returning in full force. "You should not have to save my life."

She propped her head on her hand, her expression bewildered. "Why? Because I'm a woman?"

"Because I am...I *was*...a Prince of Hell, my power

unmatched by all except Lucifer himself." I pushed to sitting and swung my legs over the side of the bed, my back facing her.

"We must continue our quest." I reached for the clothing on the bedside table. "Tell me what you saw in your vision at the temple."

"Hold on." Cinder rose to her knees and slid her arms around my chest, pressing her front to my back. Warmth radiated through the thin fabric of her shirt, and I froze, my body unwilling to end the close contact.

"I have debts to collect." My voice sounded gruff, even to me. "Lucifer and his lot will pay for what they've done to you."

"What did I tell you about acting like I'm a damsel in distress?"

I laughed dryly. "This time, it was I who needed saving."

"And next time, it'll probably be me, so let's take a moment and enjoy the peace in this invisible house. It could be our last chance to breathe." She released me, moving to my side and sitting cross-legged next to me.

A soft smile tugged at the edge of her lips, a stark contrast to the gravity of our situation.

I exhaled, tension easing from my shoulders. "I promise to see you home safely, but..."

"I know." Her gaze lingered on me, sharp and steady as always, daring me to look away. Silence stretched between us, words unspoken saying everything we needed to say. She felt our bond as I did... worried about the inevitable. Even if we made it out of Hell alive, neither of us would survive our parting.

"What did you see at the temple?" I asked again, quieter this time.

Cinder's eyes darkened, the memory of her vision flickering in their depths. "Hecate in chains. I couldn't tell if they were real or metaphorical, but she's in pain."

A chill bristled along my spine, hope and dread mingling inside me. "Do you know where to find her?"

"I ran out of time. I'll try scrying again in a bit, but..." She shook her head.

"But...?" I angled toward her, and her gaze bounced from my exposed manhood to my face and back again. "My nakedness still bothers you?"

Her lips parted, but she missed a beat before she replied. "No. I've seen plenty of dicks in my life. Yours is nothing special."

It twitched, and her cheeks flushed. Nothing special, indeed.

I suppressed a smile and pulled the sheet into my lap. "You said you could scry, but...?"

She blinked twice, the tension in her posture easing. "You're not the only one whose powers are out of whack."

My jaw tightened, a sense of unease settling in my chest. "Elaborate, please."

"My persuasion magic didn't work when I went shopping, and I had to fight a centaur to get out of the store. My fire isn't working right either." She lifted a hand and dropped it into her lap, the gesture defeated.

Anger simmered in my gut. Toying with my magic was insult enough, but Lucifer had no clue the wrath he would face for harming my witch. My soulbride.

"I will ensure Lucifer's demise is slow and relentless for what he's taken from you." I shot to my feet, fisting my hands as I paced the length of the bed. "How dare he strip your powers? His head will be the one on a stake."

"I'm not sure he's the one who did it," she said.

I continued my rant. "He thrives on toying with others' lives. Everything is game to him, but this time, he's gone too far. This time, I will make him pay. I will raze the entire Underworld in your name."

"Hey." She clasped my hand, lacing her fingers through mine. "As hot as it is that you want to burn the world for me, I have another theory. Sit down."

She tugged me to the mattress, and I obeyed her command despite the inferno raging inside me.

"Lucifer isn't responsible for my misfiring magic," she said. "You are."

I snapped my head toward her, my eyes narrowed. "I would never harm you."

"Maybe not on purpose." She sandwiched my hand between both of hers.

"Explain," I demanded, though my voice came out softer than I expected. Her grip was warm, grounding me, pulling me back from the brink of wrath.

She searched my eyes, inhaling deeply before speaking. "Our bond is doing it. My soul, my magic is tied to yours, like yours is to mine."

I stared down at our joined hands, the pulse of energy beneath her skin subtle but undeniable. "Fate willed the bond we share. It would not cause you harm."

"Again, not on purpose. But think about it. When Seraphine hit me with a poison arrow, you felt the effects too. Not because you were hit, but because our souls are bound."

"You're saying the stripping of my powers is inadvertently affecting yours?"

She nodded. "At the temple, you tore through Lucifer's magic and called on your demon, but it wiped you out. You were sound asleep, still recovering, when I tried to call on my persuasion and fire. I couldn't access my magic because my soul is part of yours now."

A heavy silence settled over us, realization hanging in the air. Her strength waned when mine did. I tried to steady my breath, but guilt gnawed at the edges of my resolve.

"So every time I falter, you suffer," I whispered, shame flooding my voice.

"It works both ways." She squeezed my hand. "That's the price of a soul bond, isn't it? We can't live without each other."

My chest tightened. "I would never wish this on you."

She smiled sadly. "Neither would I, but here we are. I didn't mean to connect us like this. If anyone is to blame, it's me."

"I'll find a way to break the bond," I said, my voice thick with emotion. "We'll find a way together."

"There's a problem with that." She leaned forward, pressing her forehead to mine and sliding a hand behind my neck. "I'm starting to like it...to like *you*... and I'm not sure I want it broken."

CHAPTER 10

CINDER

oly Hecate in heels. Did I just admit that out loud? To his face?

More like *in* his face. I don't know what came over me, but the vulnerability he was showing, mixed with his *touch her and die* attitude, had me feeling a lot more than the warm fuzzies.

Neither of us moved. We didn't speak...barely breathed...as my words sank in. Good goddess, was it true? Did I *like* being his soulbride? Did I enjoy being so connected, so much a part of another person, that I literally could not exist without him?

Breathing in Hell's sulfurous air must've affected my brain because, yes. Yes, I did.

I inhaled a shaky breath and swallowed the thickness from my throat. "Do you think..."

"I do not wish to think." He crushed his mouth to mine.

I'd like to say the kiss brought me clarity. That the moment his lips touched mine, I realized how incredibly stupid it was to fall for the fallen Prince of Hell. That I remembered I was a light witch on a mission to save my family, and that consorting with demons was not only forbidden, but it was extremely irresponsible.

Instead, I melted into his embrace, all rational thought fleeing from my mind as his touch, his warmth grounded me in the moment. Yes, our situation was beyond dire. Yes, the moment we left the safety of this sanctuary, we'd go straight back into fight or flight mode, so... We might as well enjoy the peace while we could, right? I'd worry about the consequences later.

As my last flying eff drifted out the window, I rose onto my knees and slid my hands over his bare chest, my fingers finally tracing the contours of his muscles like they'd itched to do when I first summoned him.

His skin was soft, the sinew beneath it firm, and the otherworldly heat radiating from his body wrapped around me like a velvet blanket. He moaned into my mouth, slipping his hands beneath my shirt, sliding them around to my back, and pulling me down on top of him.

He parted my lips with his tongue, and the taste of him turned my skin to gooseflesh. I pulled away, sitting back on my heels to take off my shirt as he moved to the middle of the mattress.

His pupils dilated, his nostrils flaring on a deep inhale as he drank me in with his gaze. "You are the most beautiful creature Hell has ever seen."

I licked my lips, catching the bottom one between my teeth as I straddled his legs. His body was exquisite, the perfection of a sculpture accented by the warmth and emotion of a living, breathing soul.

A soul that...at least for the time being...belonged to me.

The mossy-green of his irises billowed like smoke, his demon side also approving of the view.

Lowering to my hands, I crawled higher, hovering my body over his. My hair spilled around his shoulders, framing his face in rose-colored curtains. He held his hands near my sides, still not touching, our magical energy mixing with anticipation, swirling into a tangled knot of yearning and desire.

My heart pounded against my ribs as I lowered my head and brushed my lips to his. He groaned, wrapping his arms around me, holding me against his chest as he rolled on top of me. His breathing grew shallow, and as he used his knees to spread my legs, his pupils constricted, his heated, primal gaze stilling me, insisting I yield to his desire.

I was all too happy to oblige.

I clutched his shoulders, and he gripped his cock,

rubbing the tip against my folds. I spread my legs wider, lifting my hips and silently begging him to take me.

He arched a brow, a sly smile curving one side of his mouth. "I haven't been with a woman in over four hundred years. I plan to savor every moment of this."

He lowered, covering my body with his, enveloping me in warmth, making my core ache with need. His breath against my ear made me shiver in a good way, and when he nipped my lobe between his teeth, electricity rocketed through me.

Digging his fingers into my hair, he kissed me again, harder, more purposeful, as if this kiss could be our last. In our predicament, it very well could be.

"You're beautiful." His words vibrated across my lips before he moved, trailing kisses down my neck and circling his tongue around the dip at the base of my throat.

I wanted to reply that he wasn't so bad himself, but as he sucked a nipple into his mouth, all I could manage was a moan. He inhaled deeply in response, running his hand up my stomach to cup my other breast. My nipple hardened between his fingers, and he bathed it in the heat of his tongue before continuing his descent.

He kissed a trail of fire down my abdomen, stopping just above my sweet spot and gazing up at me, a wicked grin curving his lips. "I could lie here and feast on you forever."

My stomach fluttered, and I finally found my voice. "I'll settle for right now."

"Mmm..." he murmured before he blew a warm breath across my center.

I gasped at the sensation, my senses heightened to the point that even the smallest breeze felt like ecstasy, and when he slipped out his tongue to taste me, fireworks exploded in my soul. My hips bucked of their own accord, and he gripped them, holding me steady as he devoured me.

His moan vibrated through me, adding to the titillation and pushing me closer and closer to the brink. I closed my eyes and gripped the sheets in my fists, willing myself to hold on a little longer.

The orgasm built, coiling in my core and making it hard to breathe. Just when I thought I couldn't take any more, he dipped a finger inside me. Then a second one. My climax rocked me to my very soul. Every nerve, every cell, every fiber of my being sang as a flush of hormones surged through my veins.

But Discord wasn't done with me. He held on, relentlessly pleasuring me until another orgasm crashed into me like a wave. Before it could finish, he moved with otherworldly speed, lying on top of me and slamming his cock inside me.

We cried out simultaneously, holding each other

tightly as he filled me, his face nuzzled against my neck. For a moment, we didn't move. We lay there, joined as one, completing our union with bodies and souls. Pressure built in the back of my eyes as a thousand emotions swirled in my psyche.

Never in my life had anything felt so right.

He moved his hips, sliding out and in, the delicious friction reminding my body it wasn't done with its climax. Rising onto his hands, he gazed down at me, the possessiveness in his eyes thrilling me to my core.

I gripped his arms and wrapped my legs around him, taking him deeper with each thrust. As my climax peaked, I screamed his name, throwing my head back and riding the wave. He slammed into me. Once. Twice. On the third time, he groaned, collapsing on top of me and sliding his arms around me, holding on as if he would never let go.

Honestly? I didn't want him to let go. Ever.

I ran my hands over his back and pressed a kiss to the side of his head. A contented growl rumbled in his chest. Or was it a purr? At this point, I didn't care. All the worlds in all the realms could fall apart around us as we lay there, locked in our intimate union, both unwilling to sever the bond just yet.

Discord moved first, lifting his head, a crooked grin playing on his lips. "That was much better than doing it on the cave floor. Good call."

I laughed. "I'm thirty. Comfort is a must."

He rolled off me, tugging me toward him, and I snuggled into his side, my head on his shoulder, my leg draped across his waist. My mind began to race in the stillness. Thoughts of how crazy this was invaded my psyche, and I held him tighter, silencing them with the promise to unpack it all once I was home.

Except, going home meant I would be alone. Yes, my sisters would be there, and, if all went as planned, my parents too. But I'd have to step up and become High Priestess eventually, and I'd have to do it without Discord by my side.

"I wish we could stay here forever." The words left my lips before they registered in my brain, but honestly...? They held a shred of truth. Maybe not forever, but how nice would it be to forget about all my worries, my responsibilities, and just enjoy life for a while?

"As do I." He kissed the top of my head. "If only we weren't being hunted. I am surprised no one has found us here yet."

"There's a cloak on the house. It looks like a dilapidated shack on the outside, and apparently, once someone crosses onto the porch, they become invisible. I've watched plenty of demons walk right by while I was standing in plain sight."

He brushed a strand of hair from my forehead. "Dilapidated or not, the demons here would not leave this structure unoccupied, especially with the inside in pristine condition. Perhaps they are unable to cross Hecate's magical threshold."

"A ward. That makes sense." I slid my hand up his chest to cup his cheek. "You passed out the second we reached the porch. But if the goddess herself set it up to keep demons out, how are you inside and awake now?"

"You know how."

I propped my head on my hand. "Our bond."

"Precisely. Had Lucifer not bound my powers, we would be unstoppable."

"Even with them bound, they haven't stopped us yet." I sat up and rested a hand on his chest. "And I don't intend to let them."

"Neither do I." He clasped his hands behind his head, gazing up at me from the pillow.

A strange flutter rose from my stomach to my chest, a disbelieving laugh escaping my throat as I shook my head. Never would I ever have believed lying in bed with a demon would feel so *normal*. He had talons and horns and the strength of twenty humans simmering just below the surface, but right now, in this moment, he was all man. All...mine.

"I love your smile." He sat up and brushed the backs of his fingers over my cheek. "But your laugh sounded uncertain."

"It's just weird, being here with you. Three dozen

demons could be waiting outside in a raging thunder-storm, ready to take off our heads, but I feel so serene."

He nodded. "It's peaceful, but it's a false sense of security."

"Which is exactly why we need to keep moving." As much as I hated ending the moment, I slid out of bed and gathered my clothes. "We need to eat and scry and then be on our way."

He moved to the edge of the bed, resting his feet on the floor and clutching my hips. "Surely we have fifteen minutes to spare before we return to the madness."

Before I could utter a response, he swept me off my feet and tossed me onto the bed. Then...he showed me the most orgasmic fifteen minutes of my entire life.

CHAPTER II

DISCORD

I sat at a small table in the kitchen of Hecate's house, watching Cinder intently as she gathered herbs and mixed potions, storing them in obsidian bottles before adding them to her bag. She had tied her long, rose locks into a messy knot atop her head, and a few stray strands hung down, framing her beautiful face, making my chest ache.

Never in my existence had I been so enamored of another being.

After the mistakes I had made, the turmoil I'd brought upon her family and her coven, I was in awe of the fact that she enjoyed my presence. That she willingly shared herself with me, mind, body, and soul. I did not deserve her kindness, much less her desire, yet there she was, stealing glances, a soft smile curving her pink lips as she worked. My presence affected her in ways I never would have believed.

I refused to question it further. What fate had willed, no one could undo, and I'd grown tired of trying. Whether deserved or not, Cinder belonged to me.

"What are you smiling about?" The melodic tone of her voice drew me from my thoughts.

"I didn't realize I was," I said.

She held her thumb and forefinger close together. "Just a little bit."

I chuckled. "I am in awe at the way things have transpired."

"If by things, you mean a light witch playing house with a demon, so am I." She placed three more bottles into her bag and zipped it shut before filling a bowl with water and carrying it to the table.

The sprinkling of herbs she dropped into the water floated atop the surface, and she set a purple candle on either side of the bowl. "I'm so glad Hecate's kitchen is stocked. I left most of what I took from the seer at her altar as an offering." She arched a brow. "Then you destroyed the whole temple."

"Hmph." I crossed my arms. "I had help."

"I know. I'm just giving you a hard time." She sank into the chair across from me and shot flames toward the candles, igniting the wicks before leaning her forearms on the table. Her position pressed her breasts together and upward, drawing my gaze.

"Indeed, you are." I adjusted my growing dick through my pants.

"Down, boy." She laughed. "As much as I would like to find out just how hard of a time I could give you, we need to focus."

"Right," I said. "What do you need me to do?"

She laid her hands on the table, palms up, and curled her fingers in a *give me* motion. "I'm going to scry again, and you're going to share your power with me. That's how we found Hecate last time."

"Except we didn't find her." I placed my hands in hers, the soft, warm skin of her palms reminding me of the way her naked body had felt wrapped in my arms. "We found a trap set by Tumult. Perhaps he manipulated your vision somehow. He had been hiding, watching our adventure unfold, and waiting to strike."

"Hmm." She pressed her lips into a hard line. "Well, he's dead now, so we don't have to worry about that. If you can think of another way to find her, I'm open to suggestions."

I shook my head. Unfortunately, I had no inkling of where the goddess might be. "Proceed."

"We call on the goddess Hecate, mother of magic, ruler of the night. Allow us to find you and end our plight. As I will it, so mote it be." She squeezed my hands. "Magic, please."

At her request, I opened myself to her, allowing what little power I had left to cross the barrier of skin and seep into her psyche. She inhaled quickly at first, and then she took a deep, slow breath.

The tightness around her eyes softened as she stared into the bowl, the energy in the room shifting slightly as she slipped into the scrying trance. Her expression blanked, and I reached out with metaphorical fingers, caressing the tether that bound us, searching for her consciousness.

All I found was static. Only witches could perform this feat of magic, and though my magic helped her go deeper, I could see nothing of her vision.

Five minutes of silence passed before shouts sounded from outside. I twisted in my seat, craning my neck in an attempt to see out the window without letting go of Cinder's hands. Her breathing grew quicker, shallower, and sweat slicked her palms, but I couldn't tell if the distress came from her vision or from the commotion on the street.

More shouting ensued, along with the sounds of fists hitting bodies and the grunts and groans of those engaged in the quarrel. It was nothing unusual for this town. This place had always attracted the vilest, most unintelligent beings in the realm. It was a cesspool of the stereotypes who gave my species a bad name.

The shouting grew louder, and hoof steps clacked on the stone walk leading toward the house. It appeared, even with Hecate's magic shielding this house, we were about to have visitors. I closed my eyes and sent another pulse of magic into Cinder, hoping to speed her vision along.

"Too much," she wheezed, and I reeled it in.

"It seems we've been discovered." I attempted to release her hands, but she tightened her grip.

"I need more time."

"*I'm not going in there. That place is cursed,*" a gruff voice sounded from outside. "*Banazar foamed at the mouth for three weeks when he tried.*"

"We don't have more time," I said.

"Just a little." She squeezed me tighter and sucked in a deep breath, furrowing her brow in concentration.

"*I'll do it,*" another demon said two seconds before he let out an agonizing wail and thudded onto the ground.

"Cinder." I shook her hands, trying to bring her out of the trance. She didn't respond.

"*How do you even know they're in there?*" the gruff voice asked. "*No demon has ever been able to get close to that house.*"

"*There's nowhere else they could be, you imbecile.*" Hooves stomped on the stone, and I leaned, craning my neck again. I caught a quick glimpse of a horse's ass, his tail swishing in annoyance.

"Cinder, it's the centaur." I tugged from her grasp, and the window behind me shattered. Something hard hit the back of my head, making my vision swim, and Cinder gasped, her eyes widening as she pressed a hand to her chest.

"There's a shroud on this building," the centaur said. *"I heard glass break where it appeared there was none."*

Another object crashed through an adjacent window, and I picked it up before grabbing Cinder's arm and dragging her away from the glass.

"Why are they throwing canned meat?" I held up the culpable object.

"Long story. How many are out there? Can we take them all?" She darted toward the counter and grabbed her bag.

"If we were operating at full strength, yes. But in this condition, and without weapons..."

"Here." She reached into the bag and handed me a knife, taking one for herself before situating the straps on her shoulders.

I tested the weight of the thin, serrated blade. "This is used for cutting meat at dinner."

"It was the best I could find." She slid the curtain aside slightly to peer out the window. "Holy shit. Horse-man rallied the whole town."

I looked from my left hand, holding the canned meat, to my right, holding the flimsy knife. I could do more damage with the can.

Standing behind my witch, I peered out the window as the centaur clutched an imp and hurled it toward the house. The moment the creature hit the ward, its body exploded, slime and blood flying outward in every direction. The imbeciles cheered, encouraging the centaur, and Cinder drummed her fingers against the wall, narrowing her eyes as she watched the commotion.

"He's trying to break the ward." She turned to me as the centaur picked up another imp and threw it onto the porch. Guts splattered against the window, and she flinched. "He'll sacrifice them all to get to us, and they're egging him on. What morons. Is everyone in Hell that stupid?"

I arched a brow, silently asking her to examine her words.

She rolled her eyes. "I obviously don't mean you, silly."

"Demons possess varying levels of intelligence, the same as humans and witches in your realm."

Another flying demon bomb soared through the air, the lower-mid-level fiend making it all the way to the door before it screeched and darted down the steps, clutching its head and running face-first into a thorny bramble. It thrashed and screamed at a high pitch that nearly burst my eardrums.

"Let's head out the back." Cinder clutched my arm and guided me down the hall. "Talk about your déjà vu."

"We do seem to find ourselves the targets of

ambushes frequently." As we passed the bedroom, I cast the rumpled sheets a longing glance. Of course, our peaceful solitude had been too good to last. Perhaps one day...

A thud sounded from the front of the house, like a body slamming against the door. I spun around to find the silhouettes of half a dozen fiends darkening the windows. Hooves clattered on the stone outside, a guttural roar ripping from the centaur's chest as he charged.

"It appears they've broken the ward," I said.

"No shit." Cinder held up a hand, indicating that I should stop. "They're behind the house too."

I peered out the window. Eight more demons approached from the alley. "Is there another way out?"

"How would I know?"

"Did you not just commune with Hecate? What did she show you?"

"It's complicated. I'm still processing."

Another *thunk* sounded from the front. More glass shattered. Something splatted onto the floor. An imp chittered, its reedy voice grating in my ears before three more hit the floor. They charged down the hallway toward us, screeching like the animals they were.

I held up my hand. "Stop. Obey your prince."

They froze, their gazes cutting toward each other as they attempted to comprehend my order. "Priiiiince…?" one of them uttered, tilting his head like a hellhound who'd just heard a banshee scream.

"You will obey my command." I pointed at each of them. The first three trembled. The fourth let out a green cloud of foul-smelling gas from his backside before scratching his ass.

"Looks like some still recognize your authority." Cinder stood beside me, rocking from foot to foot and clutching a knife.

"Imps are the lowest level of bipedal demons in the realm. Their brains are the size of pebbles, and they will follow any demon's orders as long as they are fed."

"I know a few humans like that. How do we kill them?"

"There's no need. They will do as I say." The moment I uttered the final word, the front door splintered with a thunderous *crack*.

Ducking his torso to fit through the threshold, the centaur charged into the house, his crossbow drawn, an arrow already notched. The imps turned, focusing their bulbous eyes on the source of the disturbance.

The centaur released his first arrow. I shoved Cinder into the bedroom, and the razor-sharp tip clipped my shoulder. He had already notched another arrow by the time blood pooled in my wound.

The centaur surveyed the chaos—shattered glass, impish bodies, the stink of sulfur hanging thick in the air. His hooves gouged deep furrows in the stone as he halted, his gaze fixed on me, an arrow aimed at my chest. He was armored in battered bronze, his chest plate etched with runes that shimmered in the dim light.

"Attack!" he barked, his voice echoing off the walls with the authority of someone accustomed to obedience. But the imps didn't move.

"Priiiinnnce…" the flatulent one muttered, pointing at me.

"Prince?" The centaur's eyes narrowed as he focused on my face. "Discord," he grumbled and returned the crossbow to his back, exchanging it for a long blade. "I'll have your head."

"Why?" Cinder joined me in the hall, crossing her arms and jutting her hip to the side in a defiant posture. "Lucifer doesn't want a horse's ass by his side. You've got nothing to gain."

His nostrils flared. "Perhaps I'm after a different kind of reward. One where you remain alive, enslaved to me for eternity."

My rational mind shut down once again, primal instinct taking control at his threat, and I lunged toward him, plunging the knife into the exposed skin beneath his breastplate. I sank the blade so deep that half the handle disappeared into his flesh. He wailed and reared back onto his hind legs, his front hoof connecting with my head.

Splitting pain exploded in my skull. I threw the canned meat at a joint in his back leg, dislocating it. He screamed and stumbled, but his remaining three legs kept him upright.

"Wahoo!" an imp yelled, and all four scrambled toward the centaur, climbing onto his back and sinking their pointy teeth into his flesh.

He spun, his backend knocking over a cabinet as he bucked wildly, desperate to dislodge his tormentors. The imps clung to him, howling with manic delight. One gnawed on his shoulder while another latched onto his armor, scratching at the runes etched into the battered metal. A third imp scrambled up his back, yanking two arrows from his quiver before jumping off, shouting, *"impetus!"* and driving them both into the centaur's flank.

His back leg gave out, his ass slamming onto the floor, cracking the stone, as his front legs slipped out from under him and he fell onto his side.

"Must be nice to have your own minions." Cinder charged and sank her blade into the centaur's side.

"Kill the prince," he bellowed as his sword clattered to the ground.

Cinder snatched it, raising it above her head, ready to decapitate our foe, when a massive demon...a spine ripper...barreled through the door and grabbed her by the neck.

CHAPTER 12

CINDER

Well, this was quite the predicament. I'd seen Mr. Beefy in action a few hours ago, and I did not want to become his next *Mortal Kombat* tribute. His claws dug into the sides of my neck, piercing the skin with searing pain. My pulse sprinted, my arteries pulsing against his fingers with each rapid beat, and I tightened my grip on the sword, willing myself not to pee my pants.

The events that unfolded next happened so quickly, I'm surprised at the details I noticed. Discord roared, sounding half like a wounded animal, half like...well, like the Prince of Hell charging at his enemy in battle. He plowed toward us, wielding a can of mystery meat and bashing it against Mr. Beefy's head.

That only worked to piss the guy off. He tightened his grip, lifting me from the floor, the tip of his claw hitting a nerve and making my entire left side convulse like I'd stuck my finger into a light socket.

The imps shouted and squealed, but I couldn't tell if they were cheering Mr. Beefy on or if it was their battle cry as they continued their assault on the injured centaur. More shouts and footsteps sounded, the horde of demons descending upon us.

I gripped the sword with both hands, my palms slick with sweat. Discord jabbed a steak knife into the side of Mr. Beefy's neck. The fiend fumbled, his grip on my neck loosening. An imp charged, bloody teeth bared as he climbed up my body and latched on to the bad guy's face.

Mr. Beefy let me go. My feet hit the floor, and I spun, my stolen sword slicing into his stomach before I whirled toward the centaur and brought the wicked-sharp blade down onto his neck, slicing his head clean off.

The three imps on the ground cheered and scrambled toward his shoulder to lap up the blood pouring onto the stone. *Gross.*

I turned as Discord shoved Mr. Beefy into the throng, and I caught a glimpse of his intestine in someone's hand before I grabbed my demon's arm and tugged him toward the hallway.

Banging sounded on the back door, the second set of fiends trying to break in. An imp followed as I ducked into the bedroom, and I motioned for Discord to join me, slamming the door as soon as he crossed the threshold.

"Unless you have a powerful ward to cast on this space," he said, "a thin door will not keep them out for long."

"Help me move the bed." I leaned against the side and shoved while the imp jumped on the mattress like we were having a demonic slumber party.

Discord braced his hands against the headboard and pushed, sliding it aside easily and revealing a pentagram situated in a circle, etched into the black stone floor. The moment I stepped inside, blue sigils glowed at each point of the star. The magical symbols represented travel, speed, crossroads, strength, and decisions.

"Come on. This is our escape pod." I motioned for him to join me, and he arched a skeptical brow.

"How did you know where to find this?" he asked.

Crash! The back door busted open. Hooves plodded on the stone. The imp squealed and jumped into the circle, sitting its slimy butt down on my boot.

"I'll explain later. Come here." I made a grabby motion with my hand, and my stubborn demon finally joined me in the circle.

"Goddess, hear me. We're in dire need. Activate the circle with magic and speed." I clutched Discord's hand and braced myself, hoping to Hecate my little on-the-fly incantation would be enough to get this baby running.

Nothing happened.

The bedroom door flew off its hinges. Two nasty-looking demons with black teeth and snot hanging from their snouts stormed in. I recited the incantation again. And again, nothing happened. *Crap!*

The demons crossed the room in three long strides. One created an energy ball in his hands. My heart hammered in my chest. My mouth went dry, and my throat nearly closed as they growled and clicked. One eyed the circle on the floor, taking half a step backward. The other paid it no mind.

He swiped a taloned hand toward my face. I recited the incantation at super-speed. His claws hit an invisible wall of magic, and sparks filled the room with bright blue light.

My skin itched and tingled, like static electricity had engulfed me, every hair on my body standing on end. The blue light grew brighter and brighter, blinding me for a full five seconds before it dissipated.

My eyes watered as my vision slowly swam into focus. I blinked rapidly and gasped, pressing a hand to my chest as I took in the scene. A deep-purple velvet duvet covered a massive bed, way bigger than a king, and a matching rug covered most of the polished granite floor. An intricately carved armoire stood against the far wall, and a dressing table, complete with a ginormous round mirror and a silver hairbrush set, stood next to it. Orange light streamed in through a slit in the heavy curtains, slicing across the mattress before fading into the corner of the space.

"Where are we?" I whispered.

The imp darted toward the bed, but Discord caught it by the scruff of its neck before it could get slime all over the blankets. His expression grim, he set the little bugger on the floor and held his palm toward it, signaling it to stay as if he were commanding a dog.

"We are inside Hecate's private chambers...at the palace," he said.

My mouth fell open, my brows creeping toward my hairline. It made sense. If Hecate kept that house as her secret she shed—her place for alone time—of course the portal would lead right back to the palace. She could move between the two spaces freely, with no one the wiser. But that meant...

"We're back to square one." My shoulders slumped. "We should have fought our way out of the shack. If I'd known the circle would bring us here, I wouldn't have used it."

"Tell me what you saw when you scried." He opened a dressing table drawer and peered inside before closing it and moving on to the next one. "Did you see Hecate?"

"Yes and no." I sank onto a dark wood feinting

couch, leaning my elbows on my knees and wringing my hands. "I think…maybe."

"We cannot stay here."

"I know." But I needed more time to process the experience. My mind hadn't put together the bits and pieces I'd felt and seen, and gathering my thoughts felt like trying to pluck Toto out of a tornado.

I shot to my feet, shaking my head. "I don't know."

"Focus, my love." He gripped my shoulders, and a calming sensation washed through me, bringing order to my discordant thoughts.

My chest warmed, and a ghost of a smile curved my lips. "I connected with my mom. She's the one who's been guiding me."

His brow furrowed, and he released his hold. The moment he broke contact, my thoughts swirled again, confusion pushing aside my moment of clarity.

"Or maybe it wasn't her. It could have been Hecate herself…or Ruin or Seraphine." I nipped the corner of my bottom lip. "I don't know."

Discord clutched my shoulders again, his expression determined. "Who did you connect with?"

The fog lifted from my mind once more. "It was my mom. Definitely. She's helping Hecate."

"Helping her stay hidden?" he asked.

I shook my head, a sickening sensation dragging my stomach downward. "She's helping her hold the veil together. It's about to unravel, and it's all my fault."

The imp made a chittering sound, and Discord let me go to point a finger at him, shushing him. My thoughts didn't turn into a cyclone again, but the crisp clarity his touch had brought me began to dissipate.

"How did you do that?" I asked. "One minute, I couldn't tell my head from a broomstick. Then you touched me, and I didn't just know the truth, I felt compelled to tell you."

"Your magic counters mine," he said, matter-of-factly. "My power causes discord. It brings about disagreement, confusion, lies, and deceit. When I used it on you, it brought out clarity and truth."

I opened and closed my mouth a few times. "Did you know that would happen, or did you think causing discord in me would be helpful right now?"

"I knew it would have the opposite effect on you." He clamped his mouth shut in the guiltiest way possible.

"*How* did you know?" I crossed my arms. "Have you done this to me before?"

"Once, and only for a moment." He shrugged. "When I realized the effect it had on you, I immediately stopped. It never occurred to me that bringing someone clarity and truth might be beneficial."

"Because you're a demon." I shook my head.

"I am what I am."

And who could argue with that?

"When did you do it?" I ground my teeth, not that I was surprised he'd tried. My rational mind insisted it was impossible. Sure, I was a powerful witch, but to turn a Prince of Hell's magic upside down? Come on. He must've been tapping into something else, but whatever it was, it worked.

"You know what? It doesn't matter. Do it again." I made a gimme motion with my fingers. "Make me tell you where to find Hecate and my parents."

He reached for me, and the doorknob turned, making my heart take a flying leap into my throat. Discord pulled me to his chest and backed into a darkened corner behind a three-paneled dressing screen. He made a *shhhp* sound, calling the imp, and the slimy little bugger obeyed the command, joining us in the shadows as the door creaked open.

I twisted in my demon's arms to see who came into the room, and Discord must have anticipated the *holy shit* that tried to escape my lips because he clamped his hand over my mouth to silence me as Lucifer stepped into the chamber.

My body couldn't decide if it wanted to freeze or tremble. A cold shiver ran from the base of my spine to the crown of my head, and all my blood plummeted to my feet.

Lucifer walked slowly, his hands clasped behind his back, his footsteps barely whispering against the stone floor. His wavy blond hair was gelled perfectly into place, with one lock curling down onto his forehead. A hint of black painted his roots, which meant anger simmered beneath his calm exterior.

I swallowed, and Discord tightened his grip, pulling me closer to his chest. His heart pounded against my shoulder, his chest barely moving with his controlled, shallow breaths. Even the imp barely moved, though I couldn't tell if he was frozen in fear or by Discord's command.

My stomach bubbled, no doubt protesting all the strange and unusual foods I'd eaten in the past few days, but thankfully, the sound stayed inside my body.

Lucifer stopped next to the bed and brushed his fingers over the duvet. He inhaled deeply and let out a long, slow breath that sounded like the saddest, most forlorn sigh ever. My heart *almost* broke for the guy. Had he not put a price on my head and sent all of Hell after me, I would have felt bed for him. Instead, I focused on calming my breathing and ignoring the painful cramp pinching my side.

The devil needed to hurry up and cry on her pillow, beat off on the duvet, or do whatever he came in to do, because I could not stand still much longer.

He turned and sank onto the edge of the mattress. A piece of black moonstone sat atop the bedside table, and he picked it up, turning it over and over in his hands. I swear I saw his lower lip tremble, but with the lighting so dim, I might have imagined it.

Stilling, he gripped the moonstone tightly, and I did not imagine the tendons in his neck tightening like cords, nor did my mind concoct the sound of the stone cracking in his grasp as he groaned. His hair turned jet-black in half a blink, and the moonstone crumbled in his hands. He shot to his feet and hurled the shards against the wall beside us, the impact turning them to fine powder two feet from my head.

Discord went utterly still. He didn't breathe, probably didn't even blink, while I, on the other hand, sucked in a quick intake of air, inhaling the powdered moonstone along with it. My eyes watered, blurring my view of Lucifer as he whirled toward the dresser and leaned his hands on the surface. My nostrils flared, my nasal passages burning like I'd snorted a tablespoon of wasabi.

Then came the itch. It started at the bridge of my nose, spreading upward and out to the inner corners of my eyes. Pressure built. My nose twitched, the inevitable sneeze creeping closer and closer to the surface. Discord tensed, a silent warning to do everything I could to hold it in...as if the direness of this situation wasn't clear.

Lucifer gripped the edges of the dresser and flung it across the room like it weighed nothing. It smashed into the headboard, splintering, spilling its contents onto the floor and mattress.

My nose convulsed like a rabbit, and I held my breath. I would not sneeze. I couldn't. My legs trembled from standing still, and my head spun. I slowly, carefully unlocked my knees so I wouldn't pass out. The stitch in my side cramped harder.

The devil gently picked up a dark blue, satiny chemise and pressed it to his nose, closing his eyes as he inhaled deeply. His fists tightened on the garment, and he opened his eyes, his irises glowing red as he ripped the shirt into two.

He huffed and dropped to his knees, clutching two more garments to his chest and letting his head drop back as he heaved.

My entire abdomen cramped. Tears poured down my cheeks. Snot leaked from my nose, threatening to curl over my lip as itchy, stinging pressure built and built and built, my entire body tensing with the need to release it. I couldn't sneeze. My life depended on it. I would *not* sneeze.

My body convulsed, but I held it in...and farted instead.

CHAPTER 13

CINDER

The sound was short and brash like a trumpet blaring, and if that wasn't bad enough, the imp had to cackle like a hyena.

"Who's there? Show yourselves." Lucifer flicked his wrist, sending the dressing screen flying across the room, and he ignited a ball of blue flames, floating it toward us to illuminate the intruders.

Discord whispered an explicative I dared not repeat, and the imp squealed, latching onto my leg and sliming my pants. Had I not just been caught trespassing in the devil's lair, I might've been mortified. Not only had the sound of my butt trumpet been loud enough to wake the undead, but the stench it unleashed was bad enough to singe my nose hairs.

Hey, at least I'd lost the urge to sneeze.

Lucifer made a disgusted face like he'd whiffed a

foul fart…which he had…and his brows slammed down over his eyes in a menacing expression.

Oh, but his eyes betrayed him.

For one, they glistened with unshed tears. Yep, the King of Hell had just been on the verge of crying. Second, they widened ever so briefly in an *oh shit, you weren't supposed to see that* look. And third, even facing the two people he hated most in the world, his gaze bounced to the mess he'd made of his true love's room three times before he focused on us fully.

Discord stepped forward, shoving me behind him, and Lucifer wiped beneath his nose before straightening his spine. I moved to stand next to my demon—no way was he facing the devil alone—and the imp still clung to my pants, trembling and pressing his face into the side of my knee.

"I don't know whether to applaud your audacity or to remove the thorn from my side and obliterate you both immediately." Lucifer extinguished the flame and made a come here motion with his hand. "Step into the light."

Discord moved forward, so I followed.

"How about neither," I said. "We didn't come here on purpose."

My demon growled low in his throat, a warning to keep my mouth shut. You'd think he'd know me better by now. I turned my persuasion magic on full-blast and focused every ounce I could draw upon into Lucifer.

"If you let us leave peacefully," I said, "we *will* find Hecate. We're so close."

He blinked, my magic taking hold for a second before he figured out what I was doing. "Insolent witch. Your feeble little parlor trick doesn't work on me."

It did work, though, if only briefly. But it wasn't enough to stop him from flicking his wrist and knocking me off my feet. My back slammed into the wall, all the bottles and cans in my pack jabbing into my muscles as my head whipped backward and smacked the stone. *Ouch.*

Discord glanced at me and then charged at the devil. He angled his body forward, ready to tackle him, but Lucifer simply laughed and waved his arm, forcing my demon to his knees. Discord strained, his muscles bulging as he fought against the invisible restraints, but it was no use. With his powers bound, he was no match for the King of Hell.

Lucifer pointed at me and crooked his finger. A low vibration surrounded me, squeezing like a python as it dragged me forward and forced me to my knees next to Discord. The imp climbed up my back and tried to hide in my hair. I'd have swatted him away if my arms weren't magically pinned to my sides, but alas...I couldn't move. I'd have to comb out the imp's nest later.

If we lived to tell this tale.

The devil narrowed his eyes, cutting his gaze between us. "Why are you here?"

"I told you—"

"Hecate sent us," Discord said before I could finish my snarky reply.

Lucifer's nostrils flared, his posture stiffening as he focused on my demon. "You found her? Where is she?" Was that desperation in his voice? Just how hard up for the goddess was he?

"Cinder has connected with her. We were at her home in The Hollow. She'd created a travel circle there, and we used it to escape a horde of imbeciles."

"We did you a favor," I blurted. "Mr. Beefy and the centaur almost got us, but we took them out. You'd have hated to have those two idiots by your side."

The devil growled, his lip pulling into a sneer. "Where is Hecate? *Think* before you speak again."

I swallowed hard, opened my mouth, and closed it again.

"We have yet to locate her physical form," Discord said, "but Cinder has connected with her mentally. We know where to look next."

"Lies." Lucifer's pupils narrowed into vertical slits, his irises glowing in shades of molten gold. He curled his hand into a claw and swung his arm at Discord. His fingers never made contact with my demon's skin, but Discord's head jerked to the side and four bloody marks sliced across his cheek.

"He's not lying." I struggled against my invisible chains, but it was no use. I might as well have been encased in concrete.

Lucifer turned his snake eyes toward me and made a fist, using magic to grab me by the throat, cutting off my air supply like he was the real-life version of Darth Vader. "Hecate would not waste her time on a mere mortal witch."

Shadows danced in my peripheral vision, and stars began to sparkle in front of my eyes. The puncture wounds Mr. Beefy had made stung as fresh blood trickled down my neck. My lungs burned, and I tried desperately to draw in a breath, the devil's ultra-low vibration threatening to crush me beneath its weight.

"There's nothing mere about her," Discord said. "Your Highness, please. I beg of you."

Lucifer loosened his grip ever so slightly, just enough for me to inhale like I was breathing through a straw. The sparkling stars dimmed, my vision swimming back into focus, but I still couldn't move.

The devil inclined his chin, looking down his nose at me before turning to my demon. "You beg of me? After all your misdeeds, you dare beg of *me*? I'll rip you limb from limb and drink wine from your skull for what you've done."

His grip on me loosened more. I drew in a full breath and wiggled my pinkie.

"No." Lucifer whirled toward me. "You'll watch as I tear your little witch to shreds. Then, I'll lock you in the deepest, darkest prison, from which you will never escape, where you'll spend eternity in lament, knowing the price of your folly was her life."

Jeez. Dramatic much? I pressed my lips together, stopping myself from explaining that Discord would die along with me. In his current agitated state, I could practically see steam coming from the devil's ears. Best not to poke the hell bear. He'd probably rip off my head and be done with us both.

"If you kill me, I can't find Hecate for you," I said instead. "Finding her is more important than exacting revenge, isn't it?"

"I don't need Hecate. I say good riddance to the damn witch." He paced a few steps to the left, turned on his heel, and paced back. "Every action has a consequence. All misdeeds come at a price."

"And the road to Hell is paved with good intentions. Got it. But..."

"Cinder," Discord hissed, and the imp entangled in my hair whimpered.

"Think about how miserable you've been since she left." I continued pressing, letting a smidge of magic lace my words, subtly increasing my cred. "How wonderful it would be to have her back. Killing me won't fix any of that."

"Perhaps not, but watching you both pay the price for his insolence will be glorious."

"Glorious enough to fill the gaping hole in your heart?" I wiggled two more fingers.

Lucifer's hair turned blacker than black, so dark it could have been a void or even a glitch in the matrix. His nostrils flared, and white flames danced in his irises. "My heart is black as tar, and any holes are there by design."

He tightened his fist, choking off any more words of persuasion I might have tried. The pressure around me increased, the low vibration rattling all the way to my bones as he magically lifted me from the floor. The imp squealed and untangled himself from my hair before dropping to the ground and cowering behind Discord.

My feet dangled. I wanted to claw at the invisible hand clutching my throat, but he kept my arms pinned to my sides. I wheezed, trying to suck in enough air to keep me conscious, but I might as well have been breathing through a cocktail stirrer.

From the corner of my eye, I caught Discord splaying his fingers. He strained against Lucifer's magic, our bond giving him newfound strength. Whether it would be enough to fight the King of Hell's power, I couldn't say. Black spots floated in my vision, and my legs twitched of their own accord, my body protesting the lack of oxygen.

"Let her go." Discord launched to his feet and tackled Lucifer.

His hold on me dissolved, and I hit the floor with a *thunk*, my knees crumpling beneath my weight. Lucifer flicked his wrist, and my demon careened across the room, his back slamming into the wall, his feet dangling three feet from the floor.

Three deep scratches formed on Discord's neck as Lucifer curled his fingers, and blood ran down in rivulets, soaking his shirt. The imp scurried to me, latching onto my leg and sitting on my boot.

"We can help you get the amulet." I stumbled toward Discord.

"The amulet no longer exists." Lucifer flung his arm, and an invisible gust of energy slammed into me, knocking me from my feet.

My shoulder hit the wall with a *thwack*, and I bounced off, landing on my butt. Piercing pain shot from my tailbone to my neck, but I managed to scramble to standing as the imp skittered beneath the bed. "You need Hecate. You love her."

His nostrils flared, his brow slamming hard as his features morphed slightly, giving me a peek at the beast simmering beneath his human skin. "I am incapable of love."

"Incapable or unworthy?" I leaned against the wall, reaching my hand toward Discord's.

The devil glowered. "Unwilling."

He pushed his magical claws farther into Discord's neck. The wounds gaped. Blood spurted from an artery with each beat of my demon's heart.

"Hecate can rot in her hiding place for eternity." Lucifer made a claw gesture at me, and searing pain exploded on my chest. Blood seeped onto my shirt, my muscles screaming as he pierced through skin.

"Why don't you tell us the truth?" I clutched Discord's hand and focused on the sigil on my arm, hoping to Hecate he'd get the message. If my magic truly countered his, we could use it to bring truth and clarity to anyone, right?

A surge of power crashed into me, rolling through my veins and vibrating my bones, filling me with exhilaration and heat. I allowed myself half a second to revel in it before I pushed it out toward Lucifer, lacing my words with magic, both Discord's and my own.

"You should stop lying to yourself," I said. "If you really didn't care about Hecate, you wouldn't have sent us to search for her."

His brows drew together, his elongated pupils returning to circles. "A fool's errand to make the game more...interesting."

"You don't sound so sure. Is that the truth?" I asked. "Is that what's in your heart of holes and tar?"

His face contorted into a bewildered expression, and he relaxed his hands, withdrawing his invisible claws from our skin. Discord slid down the wall, his feet hitting the floor as Lucifer eyed our entwined hands.

"You love Hecate, sire. You've told me as much." Discord pressed a hand to his neck, slowing the bleeding as he healed himself. "We can find her for you."

Gray dusted the hair at Lucifer's temples. "She'll never return. A piece of her resided in that amulet, and now it's gone. Losing it to the earthly realm was the final straw."

His eyes glistened, the gray spreading through his hair as his posture softened. "I wasn't the easiest deity to live with."

"I remember." Discord laced his fingers through mine, holding my hand tightly as he sent healing energy into my chest. "But she forgave your every transgression."

"Except this one." Lucifer narrowed his eyes, the roots of his hair beginning to turn black again. "*Your* transgression she will never forgive."

I wanted to launch into a speech about how even the devil needed to take responsibility for the role he played, but I thought better of it. He needed Discord to be the villain in his story, and if it meant we'd get out alive, we'd have to oblige him.

"We have people on the other side searching for the amulet," I said. "If you let us go, we'll find it *and* Hecate, and we'll set things right."

"I told you the amulet no longer exists." His hair turned salt and pepper, and I let out a slow breath. "I, too, have been in contact with someone on the other side."

I harnessed another wave of Discord's magic and focused it on Lucifer. "With whom? If it was someone from the Boston—"

"With Scorsha Holland." He flicked his gaze to mine, and all the air left my lungs in a rush. "Your mother."

CHAPTER 14
CINDER

"My...?" I started to tug from Discord's grasp, but he held me tighter, drawing me against his side as my heart plopped into my stomach and ice flushed my veins. "You talked to my mom?"

An amused grin tugged at one corner of Lucifer's mouth. "Your father was there too, though your mother is quite obviously the witch in charge. You seem surprised. Did they not tell you they made a deal with the devil himself?"

"They... I..." Holy Hecate on a highwire. No, my mom did not tell me she was consorting with Lucifer. Hell, the only reason I knew they'd summoned anyone at all was because I'd eavesdropped and followed them.

"You abducted her parents," Discord said matter-of-factly.

"Abducted?" Lucifer shook his head. "You make it sound like a wrongful kidnapping. No, they promised me their souls in exchange for saving their daughter. I required more, and they didn't deliver. I simply took what was already mine."

"Where are they?" I asked, more growl than words, completely forgetting about our newly discovered truth magic.

"You asked for the amulet." Discord squeezed my hand.

"Demanded it, really." Lucifer clasped his hands behind his back and paced slowly. "Scorsha insisted that if it still existed, it would have been mentioned in the grimoire where she discovered the curse. I insisted on seeing said grimoire, of course, and that's when I discovered a page had been torn out."

My stomach decided to drop at that moment, and I squeezed my butt cheeks, just to be safe. "It wasn't—"

"Foolish of them to try and trick the King of Hell?" He whirled toward me, holding my gaze a beat too long before he continued pacing. "Your mother swore she didn't know what happened to the missing page. Whatever the motive for her lies, it didn't matter. She refused to produce the information, your father was of no help, so I took them both."

My hands trembled, and my stomach soured even more, bubbling and churning, threatening to bring my last meal into the conversation. I swallowed the lump in my throat and inhaled a shaky breath. "Where did you take them?"

"To my torture chambers. Where else?" He picked up a silky black shirt and ran it through his hands, a tiny twitch in his eye betraying his otherwise cool demeanor. Without our truth magic in effect, he'd donned the mask of an evil tyrant.

But I saw through it. Deep down, he hurt like... well, like hell...and I had to convince him we could ease his pain. I squeezed Discord's hand and waited to feel the rush of his power before I spoke again.

"My mother didn't tear out the page," I said. "I did, and I swear all it contained were the princes' sigils. The amulet still exists, and my sisters are already searching for it. I know you want to find it so Hecate will forgive you for what Discord did. Let us help you."

His expression faltered, his brows furrowing and rising repeatedly as our combined magic seeped into his psyche. Lucifer probably had a "special place in Hell" reserved for anyone who tried to eff with his mind, but I'd worry about that fun fact later.

He shook his head. "Discord's lover destroyed it when she destroyed him."

"She stole it," Discord said. "The amulet increases the bearer's power tenfold. She would not have destroyed it."

"And you know deep down it still exists, don't

you?" I asked. "Because it doesn't just contain a piece of Hecate. It's also got a piece of you."

"Your power to send beings across the veil," Discord said. "Her power to resurrect souls."

I tried to back toward the door, but Discord held me in place. Predators could smell fear, so I could imagine the bouquet of aromas I was putting off. I suppose showing weakness in front of a being who could literally obliterate me with a snap of his fingers wasn't in my best interest.

"It was a token of your love," I said instead of tucking tail and running. "Both of you sacrificing such an important part of yourselves... Very romantic."

The devil's eyes glistened again, and he turned away, clearing his throat. "I see you've spoken with Seraphine. I hope you dispatched of the traitorous witch with a slow and painful death."

Painful: check. The death part...? Not so much. I opened my mouth to tell him, but Discord gave his head a quick shake. The imp whimpered beneath the bed.

"Allow us to continue our quest," Discord said as he sent another wave of magic into me, and I reciprocated. The feeling of our powers mixing and melding, becoming one, was exhilarating. If our lives weren't hanging in the balance by a microscopic thread, I would have basked in it.

"Set my parents free, and they can help too." I

pushed as much magic into my words as I could. "They didn't know everything I do. Let them find the amulet and make it up to you."

Lucifer whirled toward me. "I cannot set them free."

"Why not?" I asked.

His eyes twitched, and he worked his jaw from side to side like he was trying not to spill the truth. Discord squeezed my hand, and we sent another rush of magic toward Lucifer.

"They escaped," he finally said, clenching his teeth as he spoke. "There is a traitor in my midst."

The knot in my stomach loosened. "We can help you with that too. My sisters will get the amulet. Once we find my parents, they'll tell you who helped them escape. We can give you the traitor, the amulet, and your true love."

He narrowed his eyes, cutting his gaze between Discord and me. "Your sisters will be dead soon. The veil is on the verge of collapse. Demons will descend upon your world and destroy it...if the fae don't get there first."

"We're working on that too," I said. "Ash and Ember released Chaos and Mayhem. The four of them are taking care of the veil and searching for the amulet as we speak."

"My sons are free?" A wave rippled through his hair, turning every strand jet black, and his pupils narrowed, his irises glowing gold, his lip peeling into a sneer as he pinned me with a ferocious, absolutely feral gaze. "They're free and residing with your sisters?"

"Yes," I squeaked, dropping the magic and hoping to Hecate all my bodily fluids would stay inside my body. My heart took off in a sprint, my blood pulsing through my veins with every beat, throbbing, turning to ice. "If you call off the hunt, we can fix everything."

"You will destroy everything!" Lucifer lifted his arm, and a wave of energy slammed into us, knocking us backward into the wall. We bounced off, landing on our hands and knees.

My vision swam, and I was certain I'd have a knot the size of a lemon on my head, but I managed to scramble to my feet...just in time for Lucifer to lift me from the floor and slam me into the ceiling. He held me there with one extended arm and clenched his other fist, grabbing Discord by the throat and flinging him into the opposite wall.

"I will crush you with the very gears you've set into motion." Lucifer released me to grab a drawer from the dresser he'd already destroyed. The imp squealed, high-tailing it out of the room as I dropped to the floor, and let me tell you... Granite hurt like a bitch.

Every joint in my body screamed with pain, but I rolled, barely escaping the dresser drawer hurdling toward me. It splintered on the floor with the impact, and I scrambled—once again—to my feet.

Lucifer grabbed a chair and swung it, slamming it against the wall, breaking it into twenty pieces. He threw what was left in his hands at me, hitting me in the gut. I doubled over, clutching my abdomen while Discord barreled toward the King of Hell.

My demon slammed into him, tackling him onto the bed. The frame broke, the legs crumpling as it crashed onto the floor. Good thing the imp had already made his escape.

And speaking of escapes...

"Discord!" I turned to the door, ready to run, but my demon grunted. Then he wheezed. Lucifer kneeled atop him, physically choking him with one hand while lifting his other—taloned—hand above his chest.

"If you kill him, I'll die too." I held up my hands in surrender. "And if I die, the amulet will be lost forever. So will Hecate."

His chest heaving, Lucifer looked from me to Discord and back at me. His demon hand morphed back to human, and he hauled Discord up as he stood, holding the two-hundred-plus-pound man as if he weighed nothing before hurling him at me.

That much muscle slamming into my body...in a not-fun kind of way...knocked me down like a bowling pin. Everything in my backpack—crystals, water bottles, cans of mystery meat—jabbed into my back, making me scream.

Discord yanked me from the ground, threw me onto his shoulder, and powered toward the door. Lucifer flicked his wrist, slamming it before we could cross the threshold. Discord set me down and clutched my face, looking into my eyes, silently asking if I was okay.

"No, not really," I wanted to say. I nodded instead.

Lucifer snarled, jabbing his talons into the mattress and shredding it. He grabbed everything within reach, throwing and breaking things, pounding his fists against the walls in the biggest, most extravagant temper tantrum I had ever witnessed.

He let out an agonizing wail, threw his arms to his sides, and transformed. His perfectly tailored suit turned to shreds as his body grew, his skin turning deep crimson, thick horns curling from his scalp as he doubled...maybe tripled...in size.

Discord shoved me behind his back, and I whispered, "Holy shit."

"There's nothing holy about him in this state," my demon said over his shoulder. "Try the door."

I grabbed the knob and twisted. "It's locked."

"Can you unlock it?" he asked through clenched teeth, spreading his arms to shield me from the flying debris.

"I don't have the key!" I whisper-shouted.

"Are you not a witch? Use a spell."

"Crap. Right." Excuse me for my fight or flight mode going full flight and erasing my brain. I knew a spell. What was it?

Lucifer wailed again. Claws scraped across the floor. Discord backed into me.

"Hurry, Cinder."

"Crappity, crap, crap. Oh!" I hovered my hands over the lock and recited the spell, "Iron bound and sealed so tight, hear my call and yield to might. By flame and force, I break your core. Unlock, unbar, and open the door."

I grabbed the knob and twisted. The door opened. Lucifer growled and sent a pulse of magic into us, freezing us to the spot. Pressure built around us, squeezing the breath from my lungs. Those damn stars made an appearance in my vision again, and darkness tunneled around me.

"Find her," The devil snarled, and the pressure on my body reversed, making me feel like he was turning me inside out.

I couldn't breathe. Couldn't see. Felt nothing but agonizing pain.

A flash of orange light blinded me. I raked in a breath, nearly choking on the sulfurous stench. My knees buckled, my hands scraping on the basalt as I hit the ground outside the palace.

CHAPTER 15

DISCORD

"Cinder!" I spun in a circle, the remnants of Lucifer's magic disorienting me. "Cinder, where are you?"

I stood outside the palace on a gravel path. Hedges, ten feet tall with gnarled, spiked branches, towered on three sides, the path ahead allowing me to turn left or right before another hedge blocked the way forward.

Thorns hummed with magic, the sound so deep that my heart fought against the rhythm to maintain its normal cadence. As I moved forward, the brambles closed in behind me, Lucifer's infamous Labyrinth of Lies shifting and changing, making it nearly impossible to escape.

Nearly.

I had beaten this maze thrice before, and I *would* do it again.

"Cinder, can you hear me?" I kept my voice even, unalarming, even though I fought not to tip into a panic. "I need you to remain calm. The maze feeds off fear."

Silence answered, and my heart sprinted in my chest. The hedges rustled, the pitch of the thorns' hum increasing with my anxiety. I chose the left path, turning to head further into the maze, but the hedges sensed my angst.

They grew, reaching their spiny branches toward me. One wrapped around my wrist, another around my ankle. I had ten seconds at most before the maze consumed me, turning me into one of the brainless monsters that roamed its paths and terrorized those who entered.

I inhaled deeply, picturing Cinder's mischievous smile and focusing on our bond. My nerves calmed as I felt the warm pulse of her essence, and the hedge released me, allowing me to venture forward.

"Cinder, my love. Are you okay?" I paused, holding my breath and straining to hear her over the hum of magic. Still no answer.

I powered ahead, turning right and then left, the maze shifting and rearranging, making it impossible to retrace my steps. If I knew where my witch was, I could possibly muster the strength to bend space and join her. But all I sensed from her was a whisp of her essence.

Each step I took forward echoed with my determination, my senses straining for a clue to Cinder's location. The magic of the maze pressed against my skin, thick and oppressive, but I clung to the resolve that our connection would guide me through the shifting labyrinth.

I reached the end of the path and turned right, where a half-dead shedim awaited me. Its skin, normally a mottled black and gray like burnt charcoal, had turned pale, completely ashen, and its curling horns had been snapped off, leaving only two inches protruding from its forehead. Six-inch talons extended from each of its fingers, and yellow sludge dripped from its teeth as it snarled.

I felt pity for the beast. Shedims lacked the cognitive development of most mid-level demons, but I would not wish this fate...wandering aimlessly for all eternity...on anyone, not even an imp. Obliterating the creature would be the kind thing to do, but in my human form, weaponless and in this weakened state, I chose not to fight. Finding Cinder was my only priority, so I turned to head in the opposite direction.

The hedges solidified, blocking my path. I turned to go back from whence I came, but that path had vanished as well. The shedim crept toward me, making a clicking sound in its throat.

"Stand down for your prince. On your knees." I squared my shoulders at the beast, but my attempt at control was futile. Even if I had not been stripped of my title, creatures in the maze never obeyed. When the labyrinth devoured them, they became a part of its being, losing all sense of self and free will.

"Discord?" Cinder's voice echoed in the distance. "Where are you?"

"I'm here," I shouted, my words spurring the shedim into action.

The beast lunged, lashing a taloned hand toward me. I dodged its attack, stepping to the side and using its momentum to shove it into the bramble. The thorns hummed louder, slashing into the shedim's skin as it struggled to escape. The hedge pushed it onto the path, and it snarled like a hellcat before lunging at me again. I planted my feet and blocked his attack, knocking his arm aside as he lashed out.

"What the...?" Cinder said, the sound of a fist hitting her stomach cutting off her words.

Her struggle gave me newfound strength. I shoved the shedim against the hedge, but the branches pushed back, launching the beast toward me. I stumbled, and Cinder shouted a pained profanity. The brambles reached for me, wrapping around my neck and shoulders, pulling me into the hedge as the shedim rocked from foot to foot.

Cinder let out a grunt and then fell silent. Panic flushed my veins, fueling the maze, but I refused to become a casualty to Lucifer's macabre toy. Not while my witch needed me.

I set my arms ablaze, white-hot hellfire erupting from my skin and singeing the shrubbery. The brambles recoiled, the burning thorns squealing as my demonic claws extended from my fingertips. Slicing into my restraints, I freed myself from the hedge and jabbed my talons deep into the shedim's chest, piercing both its hearts.

The beast wheezed, its eyes bulging before it crumbled into ashes. The hedge absorbed what was left of the shedim, using its remains to extinguish the fire I'd set. But my flames burned too hot.

Shades of blue, white, and green engulfed the leaves. Unable to put out the flames, the maze shifted again, withdrawing from the burning section to save itself. I darted through the opening, my legs pumping, my talons still extended as I raced toward my witch.

"Seriously? Not you too." She spun in a circle, reaching for the imp latched onto her back. "My hair is not food."

"Cinder." Relief flushed my system as I stopped in front of her and plucked the imp from her shoulder before setting it on the ground. I retracted my claws and took her arms in my hands, searching her face, her neck, her body for signs of injury. Aside from the dried blood on her shirt, she appeared unscathed.

I smiled, attempting to lighten the dire situation. "All that noise over a little imp?"

She arched a brow. "All that *noise* was over the six-foot zombie demon who wanted my brains for lunch. I killed him, and then this little shit decided having a Cinder snack was a good idea too." She pointed a knife at the imp, and it cowered behind my leg.

My hands ached, the exertion of breaking through Lucifer's binding magic taking its toll. The pain spread up my arms, and I pulled Cinder to my chest, allowing myself a moment of respite before the race began.

"Where the hell are we?" she asked, pulling away and offering me a knife.

I accepted and strapped it to my thigh. "We're in the Labyrinth of Lies, one of Lucifer's favorite ways of toying with people."

"Fabulous." She rummaged through her bag and pocketed several spells she had mixed at Hecate's house. "And the zombie demons?"

"Creatures who never completed the maze." The fine hairs on my arms stood on end, sensing the hum of the thorns before my ears registered it.

"I figured as much," she said. "How do we get out?"

The hum intensified as the hedges quivered. A vine snaked across the ground toward Cinder's feet, but I pinned it with my boot and sliced into it with the knife, severing it. The thorns screamed in response, and the hedges began their shift.

"We must move, lest we become its next victims." I clutched her hand, and we paced away from the clearing, making two lefts and a right before the rotting, animated corpse of a serpentine demon—a massive snake from the waist down, his upper half resembling a muscular human with a spiked head—emerged from the bush. The brambles shifted, enclosing us on three sides, the demon blocking our only escape.

The demon, who happened to be Ascaroth, my old friend.

"An undead end. Fantastic." Cinder tugged a small envelope from her pocket and threw the contents at Ascaroth. "Standing tall or on your knees, in the name of the goddess, I force you to freeze."

Ascaroth shuddered, his snake half rippling as he moved toward us. His ashen scales, once obsidian with amber veins, flaked off as he moved, and strings of black venom dripped from his fangs as he opened his mouth, extending his jaw much further than his skull should have allowed.

"Damn it. How can he still move?" Cinder shook the envelope over her palm and blew the remaining powder at Ascaroth. He continued his slow advance.

"He's a part of the labyrinth now. You would have to freeze the entire maze to have your desired effect." I tilted my head, studying our foe. "How did this happen, old friend?"

Ascaroth groaned in response.

"You know this guy?" Cinder clutched a knife and shifted her weight from foot to foot.

"I did…before he became this hollow husk." I crept closer to him, holding the knife behind my back. "Of all the souls to perish in this maze, I never dreamed you'd become one of them."

Ascaroth moaned, the sides of his neck distending as they filled with liquid.

"Duck!" I grabbed Cinder's arm, yanking her to the ground half a second before he spewed venom. The acidic liquid hit the hedge behind us, and the entire maze screeched, rattling its branches, its thorns growing larger and sharper.

Ascaroth struck, quick now and agile, but Cinder and I anticipated his moves. We rolled, his arms clasping nothing as his torso slammed into the ground, his fangs sinking into the dirt.

The sharp, sickly-sweet stench of venom filled the air, making my eyes water and my throat tighten. Ascaroth's body twisted, the once-familiar intelligence in his gaze drowned by an unnatural hunger. I hesitated, searching his ruined face for a flicker of recognition, some sign that my old friend was still in there. All I found was emptiness.

Cinder moved quickly, jabbing her knife into his

side, piercing his formerly impenetrable armor. Scales turned to dust as she removed the blade, but he whipped around, his upper half slamming into her, his tail snaking around her, pinning her arms to her sides, squeezing until her eyes bulged in their sockets.

I threw hellfire at his face, blinding him long enough to hide my advance. Taking the knife from Cinder's hand, I leaped onto Ascaroth's back and reached around him, shoving the blade into his upper heart.

He wailed and thrashed, slamming me against the hedge while tightening his grip on Cinder. She wheezed, and one of her joints made a sickening *pop*. The hedge latched onto me, wrenching me from his back and pulling my arms and legs outward, my body forming a letter X.

Ascaroth howled, a gurgling, guttural sound that echoed through the maze like a death toll. For a heartbeat, I almost believed I saw something—remorse, or perhaps pleading—flash in his eyes, but it vanished as quickly as it appeared, devoured by the monstrous hunger that had overtaken him.

The hedge thickened around me, pulling me deeper into the bramble, and Ascaroth focused on Cinder, unlatching his jaw and opening his mouth as if he planned to devour her.

Desperation surged through me as the hedge tightened its grip, thorns pressing into my skin and drawing blood. I gasped, straining against the branches, but they held fast, feeding off my pain. The maze pulsed with malevolent anticipation, its every shadow twisting in time with our agony.

I fought to steady my breath, sending healing energy to Cinder's dislocated joint while setting my arms ablaze. The thorns screamed, burrowing deeper into my skin. Cinder followed my lead, igniting witch fire in her palms, allowing it to lick up her arms and burn through Ascaroth's scales.

I added heat, my flames turning from blue to white to green. The hedge surrendered, shoving me out of its clutches. I fell to my knees, but this time, I did not hesitate. I hurled the second knife at my former friend, aiming for the fleshy space between his torso and where his scales began.

The blade hit home, sinking into his second heart. Ascaroth convulsed, his jaw snapping shut with a thunderous crack as the impact drove him backward. Then he froze, his expression one that asked *how could you?* before he crumbled into ashes and the angry maze absorbed him.

Cinder retrieved the knives, handing one to me and clutching her injured shoulder. For a moment, the maze fell eerily quiet, its tangled limbs recoiling as if wary of the wrath we had unleashed.

"Tell me that was the final boss battle," she said, wincing as she attempted to move her arm.

"If we can make it to the center of the maze before the labyrinth recovers, then yes." I tucked a tangled lock of hair behind her ear. "Ascaroth is the most powerful being I have seen succumb to this fate, but we must keep moving. I don't know who else Lucifer has tormented since my imprisonment."

"Well, if we have to fight again, you'll be on your own." Her face pinched in pain. "My left arm is useless, unless you can pop it back into place."

"I tried to heal you with magic."

"With magic that's getting weaker every time you use it. I felt it, but you're going to have to get physical—and not in the Olivia Newton-John way." She angled toward me, taking my hand and placing it on her dangling arm. "Lift, twist, and push."

"That sounds like it will cause you more pain."

"Oh, I'll wail like a dying raccoon, but it's the only way to fix it."

I hesitated, loath to cause her more agony. "Are you certain it will work?"

"I've done it to Ember multiple times." She braced a hand against my shoulder and widened her stance. "On three."

I lifted, twisted, and shoved her arm back into place before she could utter the first count. A string of profanities spewed from her lips as she crouched and groaned, cradling her elbow in her hand.

"I said on three." She rose, her face pinching, and she massaged the culpable joint.

"You would have tensed more if I'd waited, thus increasing your pain."

Her nostrils flared, and her eye twitched. "Thank you. Now, how do we get out of here?"

"We run." I clutched her hand, and we darted up the path. "Focus on the energy around you. Do you feel the low vibration?"

"Since the moment I got to Hell."

"Go deeper. Feel the current running beneath it." I tugged her down the path to our left.

"Whoa. That's low and slow." She visibly shuddered.

"That's the energy of the maze."

"It's everywhere," she said.

"Except for the center. Search for the void, the lack of vibration. That's where we need to go."

"It almost feels like a map."

I nodded, keeping my gaze sharp for any movement in the maze. "If you concentrate, you'll notice patterns within the vibration, a pulse guiding us." The air prickled against my skin, the labyrinth preparing to shift. "Stay close and trust your instincts. The energy can help us, if we let it."

"I'll take all the help we can get." Cinder matched my pace. "I really thought Lucifer had let us go for a minute. I thought he'd given us another chance to find Hecate."

"He has. We'd be imprisoned or obliterated otherwise."

"Then why in the goddess's name did he throw us into this death trap?"

We turned right, and the hedges shifted, snaking across the ground and forming a wall in front of us.

"One word," I said, my body tensing, preparing for whatever damned soul might emerge from the bush.

"Let me guess." Cinder clutched her knife and widened her stance. "Ego."

"Precisely." I slowly turned, expecting to find a creature behind us, but the maze had boxed us in. "His pride forces him to always appear in control, even when he's obviously spiraling. He knows he needs our help, but he insists on reminding us of his power to destroy."

The thorns hummed, and vines shot over our heads, creating a canopy above us. Leaves grew in the thickening bramble, blocking the moonlight as the walls closed in around us. Determined to devour us, to trap our souls and torture us for eternity, the labyrinth shook and grew, the leaves rustling as if in a windstorm.

I called on my fire, gathering the magic in my palm, but a vine jutted out, encircling my wrist and yanking my arm into the thicket before I could ignite a flame. The sensation of a million fire ants feasting on my flesh exploded across my skin.

Another vine snaked across the ground, latching onto Cinder's ankle and jerking her from her feet. With my free hand, I shot a stream of hellfire at the branch. The thorns squealed, and it unraveled, releasing her.

I focused my flames onto my section of the hedge, burning a ring around my ensnared arm. The bush recoiled, ejecting me from its clutches, and Cinder joined me, shooting fire from her palms.

The maze closed in quickly on three sides, but the wall we burned shuddered and screeched, inching backward as we advanced.

"Which way to the center?" Cinder asked. "Let's burn our way through."

I opened my senses, searching for the void in the magic, but the pitch at which the thorns hummed and screamed hindered my ability to find it. "I don't know. I can't sense it."

"Neither can I." Cinder extinguished one hand and grasped my arm.

The moment her skin touched mine, my senses heightened. I felt a hollow emptiness to my right, so I turned and sent flames in the direction of the sensation. "It's this way."

The maze continued to close in, the canopy lowering as the walls pressed against us. But the bush we burned was no match for our combined heat. We pressed forward, each step a battle against the writhing, angry bramble blocking our path. The air thickened with the scent of scorched arbor, and our combined fire carved a narrow passage through the chaos.

Ahead, the heart of the maze pulsed with malevolent energy, its presence growing stronger as we advanced. The hollowness called, beckoning us forward. We pushed through, burning everything around us until we stumbled into the center of the labyrinth.

Silence and frigid air engulfed us. Goosebumps pricked at my skin, and Cinder rubbed her arms. I stiffened, expecting a new wave of monsters to attack, but what entered was a gust so cold it rattled me to my bones.

A stone altar stood in the center of the void, and as we stepped toward it, the walls around us disappeared, inky blackness taking their place. A knife lay atop the table, and next to it stood an ornate, gilded vase depicting scenes of Lucifer's subjects kneeling before him.

"Is this the center?" Cinder asked, her breath coming out in a cloud of steam. "How do we get out?"

"We make a sacrifice." I eyed the ground, watching shadows dance across the stone and gather in a darkened corner. "Three drops of blood in honor of the king, pledging fealty."

"Well, get on with it then." She gestured to the altar, her gaze darting about on high alert.

The shadows undulated, gathering more darkness as they rose.

"Escape requires a sacrifice from us both," I said.

She barked an incredulous laugh. "I am not giving the devil my blood, and I am definitely not pledging fealty to an egotistical dictator."

From the darkened corner, a figure emerged, its outline shifting between solid and smoke. It turned its featureless face toward us and paused, regarding us.

"This is new." My pulse thundered in my ears, and I held an arm in front of Cinder, ready to block the shadow creature's advance.

"Friend of yours?" she asked, centering her weight.

"That beast is a friend of no one."

CHAPTER 16
CINDER

"What the hell is it?" I tightened my grip on the knife, but with the way the creature shifted from solid to smoke, I doubted a blade would do any good.

"That is a tulpa," Discord said. "An entity created from nothing but the imaginings of its master."

"A thought being. Fabulous." I'd heard about these guys. Dark witches sometimes created them to do their bidding—or so I was told. I'd never seen one in person. The magic needed to create them was forbidden in my realm. "Can we kill it?"

"The only way to kill a tulpa is to kill its creator."

I laughed dryly. "Something tells me Lucifer would be impossible to kill."

"You're right about that, but Lucifer did not create this being. Ruin did."

My stomach sank. "Ruin? As in the guy who took your place? The one who's hunting us?"

"Indeed." He inched closer to the altar.

"So he knows we're here, and he sent a shadow dude to finish us off." At least Lucifer *wanted* us to get out of the maze alive, whether he would admit it or not. Ruin only wanted our heads. "Fan-frigging-tastic."

"He knows now. Whether he knew before we arrived, I can't say." Discord stepped forward, and the shadow guy lunged, knocking into my demon and making him stumble back. "This entity is too at one with the maze to have been sent in after us. I believe it resides here."

"If we can't kill it, what do we do?" I tensed, my muscles coiling, ready to attack or run...whichever would keep us alive the longest.

"We must make it to the altar and offer our blood. It's the only way out of the maze."

"Are you sure you can't do your space-bendy thing?" Because there was no way in hell I was pledging myself to Lucifer.

"Even if I had the energy, it wouldn't work. Completing the sacrifice is truly the only way out."

"Are you sure?" I asked again. There had to be another way.

"I've navigated the labyrinth three times in the past." He stepped forward, closing in on the altar, and again the shadow man shoved him back. "Few make it to the center, so it was always left unguarded. Ruin must have created the tulpa to get into Lucifer's good graces."

"Because of course he did," I said. "Okay, here's the plan. I'll distract the tulpa so you can get to the altar. Once you make the cut and start dripping blood, I'll latch onto you. Then the maze will eject us both and we can be on our way."

"It's not that simple."

I didn't wait for him to elaborate. Instead, I waved my arms like a crazy person and shouted, "Hey, shadow man, come and get me."

The tulpa whirled around and shot toward me, arms outstretched like a horror movie ghost. I hurled a ball of fire, but it passed right through its smoky form. Its solid hands hit my shoulders, knocking me to the ground before it spun toward Discord.

"The moment my sacrifice is complete, I'll be ejected." He snagged the knife from the table. "You must do it too."

"I'm a light witch. I can't." I scrambled to my feet as the shadow plowed into my demon, pushing him away from the altar.

"Now is not the time for stubbornness." He swung the blade and lunged. The tulpa turned to smoke, and Discord's momentum sent him crashing to the ground.

"I'm not stubborn. I have morals. There's a differ-ence." I moved toward him, and the tulpa turned on me, pushing me back. "Besides, I already have a blood bond with one demon, and I am not a 'why choose' kind of gal."

Discord snapped his head toward me, the look in his eyes feral as I struggled with the tulpa. The infuri-ating monster landed a punch in my gut. I doubled over and tried to slam my shoulder into its form, but it turned to smoke. I fell through it, scraping my palms on the ground. It turned solid again and kicked me in the side.

Pain exploded across my abdomen, but I stum-bled to my feet in time to see Discord slice into his palm. The tulpa wrapped its arms around, squeezing me like a vise and doing *something* to me. My body ached like I had the worst case of the flu ever imag-ined, and my head pounded. My vision wavered as a tidal wave of fatigue crashed into me, making my knees buckle.

Discord just watched as the tulpa sucked the life out of me.

I raked in a breath, the frigid air like razorblades in my throat. I wanted to call to him, to ask for his help, but I couldn't speak. Couldn't move.

One drop of his blood fell into the vase. Two drops...

Was he seriously about to leave me behind? To

abandon me to this fate worse than death, leaving me alone to wander this hell maze for the rest of eternity?

Drop number three fell into the vase.

"Bastard," I rasped as the last of my energy left my body. Darkness engulfed me. Then, the pain ceased, and I felt nothing but emptiness.

"Cinder." A warm hand patted my cheek, and Discord's voice pulled me to the present. "Cinder, wake up."

Discord... My eyes flew open, and I bolted upright. "You asshole! You left me there to die."

Heart pounding, I scrambled to my feet, my knees wobbling beneath me, my voice taking on a shrill edge. "How could you?"

I pushed him. When he didn't budge, I pounded my fists against his chest. Tears stung my eyes, and my stomach roiled. "You left me to die!"

"Shh..." He wrapped his arms around me, holding me tightly against his chest. "You're not dead."

I couldn't tell you what came over me. I suppose it was the stress, the fear and pain, the idea that he'd abandoned me—oh, that sense of abandonment—but all my emotions swirled together at once, creating a sickening tornado inside me. Tears streamed from my eyes, and I sobbed, latching onto him like my life depended on it.

"You left me." My voice was barely a whisper against his chest.

"I didn't."

"You did!" I tried to pull away, but he tightened his arms around me. "I watched you leave."

I sobbed uncontrollably, slumping into his embrace as all the adrenaline drained from my body. My heart, my muscles, the very fiber of my being ached as if I were about to draw my final breath.

"If I'd left you, you would not be here in my arms right now." He stroked the back of my head and pressed his lips to my scalp. "I would *never* leave you, Cinder. Never. You are the light to my darkness, the sound to my silence, the reason for my existence."

Another sob rolled up from my chest, and I drew in a shaky breath, letting his words wrap around me like a blanket. The conviction in his voice told me everything he said was true. His reassurance eased the ache in my heart, but a pit formed in my stomach as the realization sank in.

I was in love with this demon. No accidental blood bond could fabricate this feeling. It ran too deep—soul deep—for it to be anything other than absolutely authentic.

His heart thudded beneath my ear, the steady rhythm calming my nerves, grounding me. I dragged in another breath, and he finally let me pull away enough to look into his eyes.

"I can't live without you," I said.

"Nor I without you." He brushed the matted hair

from my forehead. "You must believe I did not leave you. Our bond is too strong for a little labyrinth to keep us apart."

"The blood bond." I swallowed the thickness from my throat and nodded.

"Our *soul* bond." He brushed his lips over mine, tentatively at first. When I didn't pull away, he crushed his mouth to mine, kissing me like I was the final breath he would ever take.

Cradling the back of my head, he slowed the kiss, inhaling deeply as he pulled away and pressed his lips to my forehead. He gave me one more squeeze before releasing his hold and stepping back, concern furrowing his brow.

"Are you okay?" he asked.

I checked in with my body. A mild ache still lingered in my muscles, but it was manageable enough. The important thing was that he truly hadn't left me. That the knife of betrayal he'd jabbed into my heart had been nothing more than a fabrication of my mind. "I will be."

"When you mentioned our blood bond, I realized you were right. You cannot pledge yourself to Lucifer when you belong to me." He brushed his thumb over my cheek. "We are one. The maze could not eject me without sending you too. I should have realized it from the start."

"Well, I'm glad we cleared that up." I laughed and

wiped the tears from my cheeks, finally getting a grip and taking in our surroundings.

We stood outside the maze, a fifty-yard wall of thorny hedges stretching out toward the horizon. The same orange moon still hung stagnant in the sky, and the sweltering heat of Hell clung to my skin, a welcome sensation after the frigid tundra of the maze's center.

"We must find shelter so we can regroup," Discord said. "Can you walk?"

"Yeah," I said, but I stumbled on my first step, my nerves still raw from the tulpa's magic.

He caught my arm and steadied me. "I can carry you."

"I'm okay." I tugged from his grasp. "Where can we go?"

"There's a gardening shed on the other side of the maze. We can rest there, and you can tell me more about the visions you received before we were attacked." He jerked his head toward the corner of the hedge in the distance.

"We're wanted fugitives, and we're going to hide out in the king's shed?" I lifted my hands and dropped them at my sides. We'd done crazier things, I supposed. "Why not?"

"Do you have a better plan?" he asked.

"Sure don't." I laced my arm around his biceps. "Lead the way."

We made it halfway to the corner when a high-pitched chitter sounded behind us. I whirled around, knife in hand, and the friggin' imp, who'd followed us from Hecate's house, took a flying leap onto my face. He clutched my hair, sliding his gooey body up to the top of my head, leaving a trail of salty slime on my skin.

Don't ask how I knew it was salty. *Gross.*

I wiped my mouth with the hem of my shirt. "How the hell did he get out of the maze?"

The imp yanked on my hair. Then he made an *om nom nom* sound as he chewed my locks. I swatted at the little bugger, but he dodged my hand and chewed faster.

"My hair is not food." I grabbed him, but his slimy body slipped from my grasp as he kept on munching. I swear I was starting to hate imps more than mosquito fae.

Discord held a hand toward the beastie and then gestured at the ground. The imp stuck out his tongue and blew a raspberry, but he obeyed my demon's command and hopped off my head.

"Imps lack the ability to feel emotions like despair and torment. The maze would gain nothing by feeding on such a beast, so it didn't waste time capturing it." He led me around the corner, and holy Hecate.

Shed didn't begin to describe the gardening paradise that awaited ahead. I'd expected some rusty corrugated metal, maybe a fiberglass roof to let in light, but this so-called shed was bigger than my entire house, store, library, and studio combined.

Like most of the buildings in this realm, it was made of basalt and obsidian, and crimson veins pulsed on the walls, making it look alive. Gnarled, thorny bushes with blood red flowers wrapped around the structure, and a walk made of crushed stone—or was that bone?—led to the double-door entrance.

We walked up the path, but Discord stopped short, holding up a hand. "Do you feel that?"

To our left, the energy in the air thickened, the static charge making my arm hairs stand on end. A faint orange line appeared in the disturbance, and as it grew, it seemed to create a vacuum, drawing me toward it.

"What is that?" I took a step, but Discord caught my arm.

"That is a rift. A tear in the veil that separates our worlds."

"I know what a rift is." I'd just never *seen* one. They were always invisible in the earthly realm.

"Good. Then you also know every demon within a ten-mile radius will be drawn to it. We must get inside before we are discovered." He dragged me three more steps up the walk. "And, no, we would not survive if we tried to pass through it. The only way to save your life is to find the amulet."

"Yeah. Okay." I followed him, even though I really, *really* wanted to try my chances with the rift. "My sisters could be right on the other side."

"And if you enter the rift, you will be torn to shreds...obliterated in the most painful way imaginable." He pulled open the door, and the imp skittered inside.

Well, that didn't sound very fun.

I followed him into the shed and gaped in wonder. Rows of gleaming stygian steel tools lined the walls, each one meticulously arranged on hooks that seemed custom-made for their shapes. The air smelled of jasmine and skunk weed—a sickly-sweet combination—and shafts of moonlight filtered through stained glass panels, casting swirling colors across a workbench cluttered with seeds and potions. It was clear this shed belonged to someone who took both magic and gardening very seriously.

"Hallelujah. Indoor plumbing." I paced toward a sink while Discord bolted the door. The water stunk of sulfur, like everything else in this realm, but it smelled better than the imp slime coating my face and hair.

I did my best to rinse it all off before working out the tangles with the wide-toothed comb I'd lifted from the discount store. When I was as clean as I could get, we settled at a wrought-iron table and dined on protein bars to refuel. I tossed a piece to the imp, and he devoured it in one bite.

"You said your mother is helping Hecate hold the veil together." Discord tossed the wrappers into a bin and returned to the table. "What did you see? How did you connect with her?"

"I'm not sure. I think being in Hecate's house amplified my abilities." It was the only plausible explanation my scattered brain could come up with.

"That makes sense," he said. "But how is the thinning veil your fault? It always wanes near All Hallows' Eve."

"Not like this. When I summoned you, the fabric began to unravel. When we both crossed into Hell, it made it ten times worse." I rubbed my forehead. "Then my sisters…"

"They summoned my brothers, weakening it even more." He curled his hands into fists. "Do you think your sisters are cooperating? Are they looking for the amulet?"

I wanted to say absolutely. That I'd asked them to do it, so of course they were looking for it. But *I* wasn't the one who'd asked them. Discord had been so cryptic in his request, and they'd probably had no clue I was right there when they'd summoned.

"I need to send them a message. Something in my handwriting, so they'll know it's really from me."

"You don't believe they took my request seriously?" He arched a brow, a hint of his former regalness playing on his *how dare they disobey me* expression.

I laughed. "If you think I'm stubborn, you should meet Ember. And Ash is overly cautious. They don't even know I'm still alive."

He lifted a finger. "Technically—"

"Do not demonsplain right now. I know I'm *technically* not alive." I shot to my feet and paced toward a counter where a quill pen sat next to an inkwell. "The imp can pass through the rift outside, right? His magic is weak enough."

"Yes..." Discord tilted his head, studying me.

"And you can order him where to go when he gets to the other side?" I opened the ink and dipped the quill.

The little beastie found the bulb for some goddess-knew-what kind of plant and chomped into it. He made a disgusted face and spat before picking up a thick book and biting a chunk from the spine.

"I can indeed, but their behavior is erratic at best," Discord said. "Are you planning to use the imp as a messenger?"

"Yep." A notebook filled with gardening records lay next to the inkwell. I tore out a blank page and wrote a letter to my sisters.

Ash and Ember,

I'm afraid the imp might devour my message before it gets to you, but I have no other way to send it. Halloween will be here before we know it, and the veil has already become too weak to bear its natural thinning. We're doing everything we can to keep it intact, but even the goddess can't hold it forever. There's an amulet somewhere on your side. You have to find it and summon Discord so he can return it to its rightful owner. I can't come home without it.

Blessed be, Cinder

I blew on the ink, helping it dry before rolling up the parchment and cutting a piece of twine from a spool. "Here, impy, impy. I've got a job for you, you slimy little twerp."

CHAPTER 17

DISCORD

"Through the rift and straight to my brothers." I tightened the twine around the imp's leg, securing the small slip of parchment to his body. "Do you understand?"

He made a chittering sound and saluted before scampering off the table and waiting at the bolted door.

Cinder crossed her arms over her chest, holding on to her shoulders and raising a skeptical brow. "Do you really think this will work?"

"Under the circumstances, I believe it's our best course of action." I unlocked the door and rested my hand on the lever. "He'll find them. Your sisters will get the letter...as long as they don't vanquish him before he can deliver it."

She cringed. "That I can't guarantee."

"The imp will do his best." I cracked open the door, blocking the imp's exit with my leg while assessing the situation. Eerie, unnatural silence greeted me. How odd, considering a large rift lay six yards away.

Ember rested her hands on my back, rising onto her toes to see over my shoulder. "I thought you said every demon in a ten-mile radius would be clambering to get through the rift."

"Normally, they would. The gardens must have some kind of ward keeping them away."

"Or they're all scared of getting thrown into the maze of misery and having to battle a tulpa." She removed her hands from my back.

I immediately missed their warmth. "I suppose that could be it. I'll see the imp safely to the rift. Wait here."

Before she could protest, I slipped out the door and closed it behind me. I scanned the scene, expecting any manner of monster to dart from the shadows. Nothing moved. Not even the air.

"This is where we part, little one. Good luck on your journey." I gestured to the rift, its edges glowing deep orange.

The imp chittered, dancing in front of the tear as if I'd gifted him an endless buffet of meat and parchment. I lifted him to the rift's level and pinned him with a pointed look.

"Do not let me down." I placed him inside the rift,

and he vanished through the veil with a soft pop. The tear closed, leaving behind a faint shimmer of magic and the lingering woodsy scent of the earthly realm.

I returned to the shed and found Cinder leaning against the counter. Moonlight filtering in through the clear glass ceiling caught on the rose strands of her hair, haloing her in warm luminescence. My chest ached at the sight.

She had no business shining here, lighting up my life...and yet, she did so without effort, with nothing more than her presence.

"I set up a ward on the shed," she said. "Hopefully, nothing with ill intent can get inside. An alarm will sound if they do." She rested her hand on the counter, tipping her head back and closing her eyes.

"Sending the imp was an excellent plan." I placed my hand atop hers.

Her fingers twitched beneath mine. "Was it? Or did I just weaken the veil even more?"

"Imps are the lowest level of demon. A dozen could slip through a rift at once without causing the veil harm." I lifted her hand, cradling it in both of mine, my heart aching beneath the intense emotions I felt for her.

"Everything I do seems to make things worse. Our literal job in my realm is to vanquish the beasties that get through from yours...and I just sent one after my sisters. What if he hurts them? Or eats their hair while they sleep? I keep screwing up." Her voice trembled on the last word. "And I have no idea what to do next."

I caught her chin, lifting her face toward mine. "You're not alone in this. You never will be."

Her breath hitched, and for a heartbeat, neither of us moved. Then she leaned into my touch, and the space between us dissolved.

The kiss started soft—hesitant, testing—but it deepened like a spark catching tinder. I slid my hands up her arms, feeling the pulse of her magic beneath her skin. When she pressed closer, the world narrowed into nothing but warmth and heartbeat and need.

Hell itself could have crumbled around us, and I might not have noticed.

"I don't want to be alone," she whispered against my lips.

"I know." I slid my fingers into her hair and pressed my forehead to hers. "You will always have me. I belong to you, Cinder. Now and forever."

Her eyes shone in the moonlight, glistening with the beginnings of unshed tears, her stoic mask of High Priestess slipping away, raw vulnerability taking its place. The trauma she had endured in my realm would have crushed anyone else.

Yet here she stood, her hands clasped behind my neck, a symbol of beauty and power and determination unmatched by even the goddess herself.

I kissed her again, harder this time, with a ferociousness I could not control. A possessive growl rumbled in my chest, and her skin turned to goose-flesh at the sound. She pulled me closer, pressing her body against mine, making every fiber of my being ache with need.

I drank her in, reveling in the tightness of her embrace and the softness of her tongue. She slid her hands beneath my shirt, and the feel of her skin against mine made my entire body shudder. I yanked off the garment, tossing it onto the counter before continuing to explore her mouth with my tongue.

She ran her hands up my chest and then down my stomach until her fingers found the button on my pants. She popped it open and plunged her hand beneath the fabric, gripping my cock and stroking it as we kissed.

What little blood I had left in my head rushed to my groin, hardening me even more, and I moaned as she set every nerve in my body ablaze.

"I need you, Discord," she said, pulling away and looking into my eyes as she unbuttoned her pants. "Now."

"Then you shall have me." I gripped her hips and turned her around to face the counter before working her clothing down her legs.

She leaned forward, jutting her backside toward me, giving me access to all her glory. Taking my cock in my hand, I rubbed the tip against her wet folds. The sensation sent a wave of electricity rocketing through my body, making it impossible to hold back.

I sank deep inside her, pulling her hips toward mine, filling her completely, and reveling in her gasp of pleasure. Stilling, I pressed into her, neither of us moving as we basked in the sensation of becoming one.

She tightened around me, squeezing me, and my dick twitched inside her. She groaned and ground her backside against me, tilting her hips left to right, up and down, before pulling away until only my tip remained inside her.

I slammed into her, thrusting hard, my rhythm increasing with each forceful pulse of my hips. She cried out, invoking both the goddess and my name as she climaxed, and it was the most beautiful sound I had ever heard.

I continued thrusting, taking her as my own, over and over. Our breaths turned to pants, our magic pulsing between us, mingling and melding, increasing the strength of our bond. With three more thrusts, I found my release, spilling into her as I leaned forward and wrapped my arms around her waist.

We stayed there for a moment, our breathing slowing, our hearts returning to normal rates. I was loath to break our intimate union, yet I knew we couldn't stay there forever. I pulled out, and she turned toward me, her gaze filled with so much passion, I nearly crumbled.

"I love you, Cinder Holland," I said, tucking a strand of hair behind her ear.

"Discord, I…" She caught her bottom lip between her teeth.

"You don't have to say it." I brushed my thumb over her cheek. "Just know that I mean it."

"I should. I do," she whispered. "But the moment I say it out loud, it becomes real."

I smiled slowly, warmth spreading through my body. "Then let it be real."

"I…"

The moon's faint glow filtering through the ceiling shifted. The garden, which had been silent and still moments ago, now shimmered with movement—leaves rustling without wind, branches cracking and growing, snaking across the roof in a tight lattice.

Cinder frowned and drew away from me, pulling up her pants. "Do you feel that?"

The hairs on my arms rose as I followed suit, the shifting energy growing palpable around us as we dressed. I crossed to the door, cracking it open to peer out. What had been a tangle of dying vines an hour ago now crawled with life, thorned stalks glistening like glass, their tips catching the faint orange of Hell's sky. As they moved, they made a sound like whispering voices, just beyond hearing.

"Stay here," I said as I stepped outside.

Cinder followed me out the door. "Those weren't there before."

"No." I drew the knife from my belt, the ground crunching beneath my boots as I inched forward. The plants shimmered as I moved closer, their translucent petals reflecting my face back at me.

Cinder joined me, resting her hand lightly on my arm. "What kind of plants are those?"

"Not plants." I crouched, brushing a fingertip against one of the stems. It was cold. Too cold. A pulse shivered through it, echoing like a heartbeat. "They're grown from energy. From tortured souls."

As if in answer, one of the blossoms opened. Inside, faint and fragile, was a face screaming silently behind a thin layer of crystal.

Cinder gasped, stepping back. "Good goddess…"

The whispering rose to a hiss, the voices overlapping in tones of grief and fury. The vines trembled, reaching toward Cinder's light like starving animals.

I moved between her and the nearest stalk, drawing on the infernal fire within me. "Back to the shed."

She hesitated. "We can't just—"

"Now."

The vines surged, scraping against the ground. I shot a wave of fire toward the nearest cluster, and it erupted in flame, the glassy surfaces shattering with shrieks that faded into echoes.

Cinder's magic flared beside me, pulsing in rhythm with mine—unintentional, instinctive—like two halves of a single heartbeat. She hurled a ball of witch fire at a tangle of vines, shattering the crystal leaves, the trapped souls screeching in agony as the branches retreated.

Heat flickered along my arms. The air was thick with the scent of scorched earth and bitter magic, each shattered blossom releasing a wisp of sorrow that drifted away on the wind. Cinder stumbled back, her form outlined by the blaze, and I could see the fear and resolve warring in her eyes as the remaining vines recoiled, their whispers dimming to a mournful hush.

I moved toward her, and she touched my shoulder. "They're people. They're alive," she said softly.

"They're damned, and we'll join them if we stay out here."

She nodded, though her gaze lingered on the quiet vines. Together we turned toward the shed, but before stepping inside, I glanced over my shoulder. Beyond the blackened soil, deeper among the twisted trees, something moved...a shadow separating from the darkness. For a moment, I thought I saw eyes like shards of polished glass watching us. Then, they vanished.

I bolted the door and pulled Cinder close.

Her heart still pounded in her chest. "We have to free them."

"Their fates are not our concern," I said. "They'll devour us for attempting to help."

She drew in a shaky breath. "Lucifer is one sick, effed up bastard."

"I won't argue with that, but this addition to the garden was not his creation." My expression darkened. I knew of only one demon who possessed this sort of power. "Ruin did this."

"How did I know you were going to say that?" She sighed and stepped out of my embrace. "And why do I get the feeling that was nothing more than an opening act?"

"How long will your ward hold?"

"A couple of days against witches in my realm. Here, against Ruin?" She shrugged. "No clue. I've never needed to ward against a demon that strong."

"Search the shed for weapons." I eyed the machetes and gardening shears hanging on the wall. They'd do no good against a tulpa that could turn into smoke, but if we could make it through to Ruin, I would have his head.

Cinder tossed me a tool belt, and as I stocked it with as many sharp objects as it would hold, the faint whisper of the living vines outside grew into a murmur and then a hum. I paced toward the door, and it rattled on its hinges.

"That didn't take long." Cinder strapped on a belt of tools as the humming vines began to screech. "All those poor people."

"Careful," I said. "Compassion in Hell will get you killed."

The door rattled again. Something heavy and solid slammed into it. I leaned my shoulder against it, and Cinder drew a trowel in one hand, a machete in the other.

"If only Chrys were here," she said.

I didn't ask her to elaborate. The screaming vines snaked toward the shed, and something thudded on the roof above us. The lattice retreated, showing us the being Ruin had sent to attack.

She squatted on the roof, resting her hands in the cleared space and leaning down to peer at us through the glass. The woman wore a black dress, reminiscent of the time I'd spent in the earthly realm, and her sneer was one of pure malevolence. My heart dropped into my stomach before a spark of rage ignited in the core of my being.

"Who is that?" Cinder asked, clutching her makeshift weapons tightly. "Another friend of yours?"

"That," I growled, "is Isabel."

CHAPTER 18

CINDER

"Isabel, as in the bitch who cursed my bloodline?" I tightened my grip on the machete, anger making my blood burn in my veins. But anger wasn't the right word. Resentment, maybe fury. No...

What I felt was pure rage.

"The one who tricked me, stole the amulet, and locked me in the dark prison for four centuries." Discord fumed, his voice dripping with malice as his muscles tensed. "The reason for all our strife."

Isabel grinned wickedly through the glass. Too many teeth filled her smile, sharp and pointed, erasing what little humanity she might have possessed. She rose to her bare, calloused feet, a tattered black skirt billowing around her ankles as she lifted a leg and stomped on the roof.

The glass cracked around her heel, fissures jutting in every direction, and Discord and I backed away. She stomped again, fracturing the roof even more. As she lifted her foot a third time, I dove beneath a table.

She shattered the glass. The entire roof crashed down around us, and I shielded my face against the shards as the most wicked witch of all descended upon us.

Discord did not follow my lead. He stood there, stance wide, ribcage expanding and contracting with his forced breaths, his skin bloodied from the raining glass.

Isabel floated to the ground, her bare feet landing in a pile of broken shards. She twisted, bending her body at an unnatural angle to sneer at me beneath the table, and the glass crunched. She winked and straightened, stepping toward my demon, and I expected her to leave a pool of blood where she had stood.

A few shards stuck in the soles of her feet, but she didn't bleed. Not even a little.

Discord let out a guttural roar and charged toward her. I scrambled from my hiding spot as his fist connected with her jaw. Her head jerked back, but her wicked grin widened, amusement dancing in her solid black eyes.

She hit back, landing an uppercut to his chin and pissing me right the eff off. The sound of his lower teeth slamming into his top made *my* jaw ache, and I wasted no time letting her know. I lunged forward, jabbing the machete into her back with enough force for the blade to protrude from her chest.

I yanked it out, ready for her to fall to her knees so I could take off her head, but she just stood there, her laugh too deep, too distant for it to be her own.

And my machete? Not a single speck of blood. That pissed me off even more.

I spun and swung, the blade passing through her neck with little resistance. The action should have lobbed her head clean off, but it didn't even leave a scratch.

"I will torture your soul for all eternity for what you've done." Discord drew a claw-like tool from his belt and slashed at her chest. She laughed harder, and he tackled her.

"You seduced me. Humiliated me. Stole four hundred years of my existence." Pinning her arms at her sides with his knees, he wailed on her, landing punch after punch.

Still, she only laughed.

"This isn't right." I moved behind him and hacked at her legs. Again, the machete passed through them, not even causing a scratch.

"She will pay." Discord continued his assault, his chest heaving with the exertion of pommeling his sworn enemy.

I put the trowel back on my belt and laid a hand on his shoulder. "I don't think that's her."

"Of course it is." He jabbed the claw tool into her throat.

"No, Discord. Feel her energy. That's not a witch. That's nothing that was ever alive. She's a tulpa."

Isabel's menacing laugh deepened, and she turned to smoke beneath him, reforming on her feet, her image shimmering with demonic magic.

"You're smarter than you look, foul witch," she said in Ruin's voice.

Discord stood, his hands curling into fists, the tendons in his neck taut and protruding. "You dare toy with me?"

"You make it all too easy." She...*he*...laughed again. "You're weak and pathetic, and when you're out of my way, Hell will be mine."

Discord's eye twitched. "I'm only weak because my powers are bound."

"Even at full strength, you could never beat me."

My demon crossed his arms, his voice deepening with malice. "Tell that to Bedlam and Tumult."

"We could join forces, you know." I interrupted their pissing match, laying my persuasion magic on thick. "Help us find Hecate and return her to Lucifer. She's what he really wants."

The tulpa threw its head back, Ruin's villainous laugh echoing inside the shed. "I don't give a damn what he wants. His so-called love for that witch has made him weak as well. He sent you on a fool's errand, and once you're dead, I'll take him down too."

"You're planning to overthrow the devil himself." Now it was Discord's turn to laugh. "Talk about a fool's errand. You've lost half your team already."

"There's only room for one at the top." The tulpa shrugged. "I'd have destroyed them myself if you hadn't."

"We can help you." I laced my words with another wave of magic. "Hecate is pissed at Lucifer too. Help us find her, and she'll help you destroy him."

The tulpa looked at me, its expression thoughtful as my magic took hold. Then it shook its head. "I know where she is."

"Then show us." I grasped Discord's hand, squeezing it twice and hoping to Hecate he got the message. It was time for a little truth magic. "Take us to her, become our ally, and we'll help you overthrow your dickhead...dictator."

My demon understood the assignment. A surge of magic washed through me, and I opened to it, sending my power into him, countering his discord and forcing the truth.

"Where is she?" we asked in unison. "Tell us now," Discord added, sending another pulse of magic toward the tulpa.

The being inclined its chin. "I buried her."

A hollow pit formed in my stomach. The goddess wasn't dead. She couldn't be. "Buried her where? Show us."

The tulpa flashed its pointy teeth, lowering its chin in a blood-curdling expression. "With pleasure."

The entity turned into smoke and shot upward, disappearing into the sky.

My breath came out in a rush, the only sound penetrating the unnatural quiet, and Discord tensed, stilling, listening...sensing. We waited. And waited. Nothing happened.

"Maybe our magic doesn't work on tulpas," I finally said.

"It should have." He cut his gaze around the room. "Filtered, maybe, so not at full strength, but his tulpas are a part of him."

The tension in my shoulders eased. "Tumult's tulpas weren't nearly as scary; they couldn't actually touch me. I guess Ruin's had more practice."

Discord shook his head. "Tumult's power was illusion. He could not bring beings into existence like this."

"Can you?" I hung the machete on my belt and tugged from his grasp.

He glanced sideways at me. "Before I was disgraced, yes, I could. But I've always preferred to face my conflicts head-on, in person."

"Yeah, I've noticed a thread of cowardice running through the devil's new crew."

The moment I uttered the words, the ground shook beneath our feet. Discord clutched my arm and dragged me to his side as a three-foot-wide fissure opened in the center of the shed. The ground fell away, and the walls shuddered, the tools hanging on them clattering on the floor. The reek of sulfur and decay permeated the air, and I suppressed a cough as we backed away.

I would never get used to the smells in this realm.

As the earthquake settled, silence engulfed us, and a shaft of red-orange light glowed from below. I stepped toward the crevice, and Discord moved with me, tightening his grip on my arm as if he planned to haul my butt out of there at the first sign of movement.

I peered into the opening and let out a low whistle. "What level of Hell is that?"

Black rock extended thirty feet down on both sides of the fissure, with crimson and violet crystals shimmering and pulsing like living glitter. At the far end of the shed, a stone staircase spiraled into the depths.

"That is not a level of Hell I'm familiar with." Discord stepped back and slowly made his way toward the staircase. "It's something entirely new."

"Something Ruin created." I followed him, inching along the outer edge of the crevice.

"Most likely." He frowned, his eyes calculating. "Do you sense Hecate down there? Can you connect with her?"

"Between the scorching heat, the nasty stench, and the weird vibrations, my senses are on overload," I said. "Anyway, I don't think I ever did connect to the goddess. I think it was my mom the whole time."

"It seems we'll have to check it out ourselves." He gestured to the steps.

I eyed the staircase and curled my lip. We'd used our newfound truth magic on Ruin's tulpa. If it had worked on him like it had on Lucifer, he must be showing us the way to Hecate, but I couldn't ignore the foreboding feeling settling in my stomach like a brick of leftover meatloaf. "It could be a trap."

Discord laughed dryly. "It most likely is. Do you have a better plan?"

"Sadly, no." I shrugged. "Down we go."

He nodded solemnly. "Stay close, senses sharp."

"Got it," I said. "And kill anything that moves."

We descended slowly, our steps cautious. It wouldn't have surprised me if the staircase crumbled beneath our feet and we plummeted into the depths. Thankfully, that didn't happen.

Halfway down, the energy around us thickened. The crystals in the walls vibrated, creating a high-pitched ringing noise that felt like it came from every-where, including the inside of my head. It rattled my teeth, and I ground them together to keep them from falling out of my mouth.

Discord stopped on the bottom step and ignited hellfire in his hand, illuminating the underground chamber. The walls were made of packed earth, with slabs of obsidian that reflected the firelight. Gnarled roots protruded from the dirt, snaking toward the sheets of volcanic glass and forming intricately woven frames around them.

Ahead of us lay a pool of dark purple water, so dark it was nearly black, its placid surface so still that it could have been another sheet of glass. A series of roots extended into the pool, their thorns humming in the same mournful pitch as the vines we'd fought above.

"It's too still in here." I rested my hand on Discord's shoulder.

"Most traps are." He placed his on top of mine. "The calm before the storm. Shall we continue?"

"What else are we going to do? The only way out of this mess is through." Even though every cell in my body screamed *danger! Danger!*

The moment my demon's foot hit the ground, the entire chamber lit up, the walls and roots glowing a greenish yellow that reminded me of the glow-in-the-dark wands we sold at our little witchy shop in Salem. Man, I couldn't wait to get home.

Discord crept forward, toward the pool, and I

stopped in front of a framed slab of obsidian, cringing at my reflection. My hair was a ratted pink mess, dark circles ringed my eyes, and my skin had taken on an ashen pallor. If I could perfect my *Living Dead* walk, I wouldn't need a costume for Halloween.

"Mirror, mirror on the wall, I am *definitely* not the fairest one of all. Sheesh." I brushed the hair off my forehead and joined Discord at the creepy pool.

"Is that water?" I asked, tempted to hop into it and have a little bath.

"Yes, but it's been bespelled." He pointed at the surface. "Look closely. Do you see?"

I peered down to find my disheveled reflection next to his. How did he still look so perfect? "I know I'm a mess."

"Look deeper, beyond your reflection." His gaze didn't stray from the pool.

I squinted, trying to ignore the hot mess express squinting back at me, and sure enough, beneath the glassy surface, dozens upon dozens of ghost-like faces drifted in a nonexistent current.

I pressed a hand to my chest. "Those are people."

"They once were," Discord said. "Now they're the embodiment of pain and torment. This water gives Ruin access to their deepest fears and regrets. He uses those, along with their guilt, to hold them, to torture them, to make them a part of his macabre garden."

"I am so glad I didn't dunk my head in there," I said.

Discord looked at me with alarm. "That would be detrimental."

"That's why I asked first."

A strange vocal clicking sound emanated behind us a moment before claws scraped across the ground. We whirled toward the attacker—a solid black, featureless tulpa with blood red eyes—and drew our weapons, but the friggin' beastie moved faster than an imp at an all-you-can-eat hair buffet.

It slammed into me. My machete pierced its gut as I fell backward. The tulpa disappeared in a cloud of smoke, and I made a giant splash in the purple people eater.

CHAPTER 19

CINDER

The pool engulfed me in thick, frigid...not really liquid. As soon as the splash I'd made settled, the gooey substance began to solidify like soft serve ice cream, minus the yummy, sweet taste. Sort of solid, sort of liquid.

It became a "soquid."

I made the mistake of opening my mouth when I fell, and the salty, bitter taste of tormented souls made me gag...but that was the least of my problems. The sludge grew colder and colder. My heart rate slowed. Every muscle in my body ached like I had the all-time worst case of the flu *and* someone had beaten me with a spiked baseball bat. What was it with Ruin making me feel like I had an autoimmune disease?

And on top of all that—the sprinkles on the soft

serve—my heart wrenched and my stomach twisted as every fear, regret, and feeling of guilt I'd ever experienced escaped the recesses of my mind and rose to the surface. All the times I'd screwed up, failed my friends and family, and made the worst decisions possible flooded my thoughts. If I wasn't suspended like a piece of fruit in a gelatin mold, I'd have sobbed.

Another splash shook the pool. Strong arms wrapped around me. My head breached the surface, and I gasped. With one arm around my chest, Discord dragged me out of the perilous pool and lay me on the ground.

I rolled to my side and coughed, my lungs burning as I expelled the bitter substance. The moment it hit the floor, it rolled toward the pool and dropped over the ledge. I sat up, and Discord clutched my shoulders, gazing intently into my eyes, searching my face and body for signs of injury.

"Are you okay?" he asked.

"Never better." I pulled my hair over my shoulder, expecting it to be either dripping wet or full of sludge, but it was perfectly dry. My clothes were too. *Weird.* "Thank you for jumping in to save me."

He returned his gaze to my eyes, his brows low, his expression solemn. "I'm afraid 'save' is too strong a word. Ruin now has access to our deepest fears and guilt. He will use them against us."

"Bring it." I rose to my feet. "I am so ready to be done with this guy."

"As am I." He turned in a circle. "I see no exit, aside from the staircase."

"Maybe this is the end of the line?" I stepped toward an obsidian mirror, but it didn't show my reflection. Inky blackness drew me closer, my gaze fixing on the swirl of blue spiraling in the center, creating the illusion of depth in the two-dimensional surface.

"This can't be all there is." Discord paced behind me. "Hecate must be here somewhere."

I narrowed my eyes, staring deeper into the swirling obsidian as an image began to form. The blue expanded, forming the silhouette of a woman with long hair. Discord said something from across the room, but his words sounded muffled, like I wore invisible earplugs.

My pulse quickened, my stomach twisting and souring as the image morphed, not into my reflection, but into my sister.

"Why did you leave this time, Cin?" Ash asked, the accusation in her voice as sharp as Ember's sword. "You made a mess of Salem and left it for us to clean up...again."

"Again?" I flinched as if she'd slapped me. "I left to find Mom and Dad. I told you that in my letter."

"Right. The letter that took me over a month to

find because you hid it under multiple layers of spells." She crossed her arms. "Because you always think you're better off alone."

Over a month? Had I really been in Hell that long? "I didn't... I don't like to work alone, but I—"

"But you think Em and I aren't skilled enough to help you. That we'll screw up whatever it is you're working on because we aren't the firstborn daughter." She narrowed her eyes and curled her lip. "Maybe if you hadn't been helping Mom suppress my magic all these years, you'd have seen how powerful I really am. You'd have seen that *I* should be the one in training to be high priestess because I'm the most powerful witch in Salem."

"What?" I blinked and shook my head, my senses coming back to me. That didn't sound like Ash at all. The voice did, sure, but my little sister was the least competitive, most humble person I knew. She would never say that.

"Step away from the glass." Discord clutched my wrist and gently tugged me back. "Whatever you see in there isn't real. Ruin has fabricated it from your memories."

My breath came out in a rush, and I swayed on my feet. "It was my sister. Ash knows I've been helping our mom bind her powers, and she hates me for it."

"No. Look at me." He tucked his finger under my chin, lifting my gaze to his. "You fear she will hate you if she finds out the truth. Ruin only sees your sisters through *your* lens. As strong as he is, he cannot see across the veil. No demon can."

My lower lip trembled, so I bit it and nodded.

"She's right," Ember's disembodied voice sounded all around me. "You've always known we're better than you. That's why you run off on your little side quests alone. Because you know we can do a better job, and that would make you look bad."

"That isn't true." I started toward the mirror, but Discord clutched my hand, holding me in place. "I hate having to do everything alone, but that's how high priestesses work. I have to get used to it."

A sob rolled up from my chest, sticking in my throat. "It's tradition."

"You act like you're better than us, but we know the truth." Ember stepped from the shadows, a fully formed tulpa with long, purple hair and black leather pants. "I will *always* be a better fighter."

She swung her sword in a figure eight, just like the real Ember did right before she charged at her foe. A sinister smile—the only thing un-Ember-like about the tulpa—curved her lips as she clutched her sword in both hands and fire erupted along the blade.

"Please don't do this." I held up my hands. "I won't fight you."

"Then you'll die." Ember ran toward me, sword blazing.

I half-expected Discord to clothesline her, but something pulled his attention away from my battle. I sidestepped my sister, dropping and kicking out a leg. She tripped and careened forward, catching herself on her hands. The sword skittered across the ground before turning into smoke and reforming in her hand.

"It was done in jest," Discord said, and I snapped my gaze toward him, where he held a man with dark hair and a goatee in a chokehold.

I didn't have time to ponder who that might be. Ember jumped to her feet and circled me, so much hatred filling her eyes. "You've always looked down at me. Ash is your sweet little sister, and I'm a piece of dogshit stuck to the bottom of your shoe."

"That's not true, Em. I love you. I love you both." I turned with her as she moved around me. "I coddled Ash a bit, but only because of the curse. Because her powers are bound."

Discord grunted, and I spared him a glance. The man he fought elbowed him in the gut, and my demon shoved him against the wall.

"Save your breath, Cinder," Discord said. "You're arguing with your own mind."

"Ember, you don't want to fight me." I laced my words with persuasion magic. "We're sisters. We need to work together."

She scoffed. "Says the *sister* who ran off to Hell alone and hooked up with a demon. Do you even consider what might be happening to us while you're getting it on with our immortal enemy?"

My heart wrenched at her words, and a sob bubbled from my chest, lodging in my throat. "It isn't like that." Except, it was, and she was right. I hadn't been trying hard enough. I should've been spending every spare second looking for our parents and finding a way home.

"I'm so sorry," I said, reaching for the machete hanging from my belt. "I failed you and abandoned you."

"And now, you'll pay the price." She lifted her sword above her head and swung it downward.

I defended, using the machete to counter her blade. Sparks ignited as metal hit metal, and Ember did her famous drop, spin, and kick, knocking me off my feet. I rolled, barely missing the point of her sword as she jabbed it into the ground.

I scrambled to my feet, and she lunged again, her blade nicking my arm as I parried. She swung, and I countered with the machete, knocking her aside. Discord shouted behind me, and something splashed into the pool.

I whirled around, ready to dive in and save him, but he stood on the ground, heaving breaths and shaking his head.

Ember screamed like a Valkyrie and ran toward me, sword blazing. I swung the machete, slicing into her gut, my heart breaking and my stomach turning. Her eyes widened, and she gripped her abdomen, tears streaming down her cheeks as she gaped at me and asked, "How could you?"

Dear goddess, what had I done? I raced to her side and rested a hand on her arm. "Are you okay?"

She snapped her head toward me, stepping away and lifting her sword. Discord plowed into her before she could strike, grabbing her around the waist and shoving her into the purple pool. She wailed and splashed, calling to me with sheer agony in her voice.

"Ember!" I rushed toward the pool.

"Stop." Discord grabbed me, holding me against his chest.

I struggled against his embrace. "I have to save Ember."

"That is not your sister." He tightened his hold. "It was a tulpa, which Ruin created to torment you with your guilt and fear. He created one for me as well."

"No." The sob that had stuck in my throat finally released, and the pool's surface stilled. I drew in a shaky breath. "She seemed so real."

"I know. Mayhem did as well." He stroked my hair.

"We are real." Ash emerged from the pool, wearing her signature black corset and fishnets. Her long, blue hair hung loose around her shoulders, and she clutched a ritual dagger in each hand.

I stepped back, tightening my grip on the machete.

"If you're real, then tell me what I gave you for your birthday last year."

"That collector's edition signed box set?" She laughed dryly. "Pointless. I'd already read the books."

Ash would never say that. She loved books. It was Ember who'd thought my choice in gifts was worthless.

She lunged, slashing a dagger at my stomach. The blade cut into my shirt, missing my skin by a centimeter. She swung the other arm, and I ducked and turned, grabbing her arm and wrenching it behind her.

"You're turning into a dark witch." Her voice sounded so much like my sister's that I nearly let her go. "First, you bind my powers. Then, you choose a demon over us and send Ember into the pool of tortured souls."

"That wasn't Ember, and you're not Ash." I spun and shoved her into the pool.

She screeched and wailed, splashing and shouting profanities I had never heard from Ash's lips. Ruin was getting it wrong, morphing the memories of my sisters into one being. Her cries turned into a melodramatic laugh before she disappeared beneath the surface.

I started to sigh in relief, but Discord clutched my arm and spun me around in time to see four beings emerge from the shadows: Ember, Ash, Mayhem, and whom I assumed was Chaos. Behind them, another six tulpas emerged. Their features weren't as pronounced, but I recognized a few coven members in the mix. The other must've been people from Discord's mind.

Another shadow took form behind them, this one massive and four-legged. Yep, bringing up the rear was that goddess-damned centaur.

"Oh, for Hecate's sake." I drew a spade from my gardening belt. "Why don't you fight us in person, you coward?"

Ember sneered, leading the crew, her eyes glowing an unnatural shade of gold as she swung her sword in a figure eight. Claws extended from Mayhem's fingers, and horns protruded from his head. The centaur reared onto his back legs, his front hooves circling in the air before slamming onto the ground.

The silence that followed was thick and oppressive. For a moment, the tulpas shifted uneasily, as if awaiting orders from their master. My hands trembled, sweat slicking the handle of my spade, but I forced myself to stand tall and meet the gaze of each shapeshifting adversary. This was no longer about memories or mistakes—it was about survival, and I refused to let Ruin dictate the story any longer.

"What's the plan?" I cast Discord a sideways glance. "I don't like our odds."

"Neither do I." He clutched gardening tools in each hand.

"Retreat and live to fight another day?" I took two slow steps toward the staircase.

"I loathe running from battle," he said, "but I believe that is our only option."

"Works for me." I spun and took three steps up before Mr. Beefy appeared on the stairs. He held someone's bloody spine in one hand, their severed head in the other, and he chucked it at me, hitting me right in the gut.

I stumbled, my foot slipping, and I tumbled to the ground. Thank the goddess I'd only made it to the third step. Discord hauled me up by the arm, and we stood back-to-back, our weapons drawn, as the tulpas surrounded us.

"There are too many of them," I said. "There's no way we can fight our way out of this."

"We have no choice." Discord hurled a pair of herb shears at one of his brothers. The tulpa didn't turn to smoke, but they passed through him as if he had.

"Their features aren't right. They're blanker than they were before." I swung the machete at the advancing centaur.

"His magic is spread too thinly," Discord said. "Perhaps we can use this to our advantage."

"How?" I slashed the blade at a tulpa that resembled Shade, our shadow witch. It passed through his neck with zero resistance.

"If they aren't fully formed, they can't—" His

words were cut short when Mayhem slammed his shoulder into his gut, tackling him to the ground.

"Never mind." Discord threw a punch, but the tulpa turned to smoke before rematerializing three feet away. My demon shot to his feet and returned to my side. "Perhaps our combined magic? Use your persuasion to convince them to stop."

"It's worth a shot." I grabbed his hand and opened myself to the rush of his energy. My entire body hummed with magic, and my arm hairs stood on end as I poured as much vim as I could into my words.

"You don't want to fight us," I said. "We aren't worth your time."

They inched closer, the circle closing around us.

"You'd rather go away and send your master to face us in a fair fight." I pushed out another wave of magic, and they paused, their expressions blanking even more. "You don't want to be here."

They all blinked once in unison. Twice. Three times. A light sparked in their dead eyes, as if their master had sent his own wave of magic into them, and they continued their advance.

"It's not working." We could never beat this many entities, even if they could be killed. "Tell me what else you know about tulpas. There must be a way to get rid of them."

"Their existence is tied to their master. He created

them in his mind, using our fears and guilt to design them."

"So we're fighting Ruin's imagination."

"That is correct."

A thought wriggled in my mind…something Ash had joked about a few months ago. What had she said? I ground my teeth, willing the memory into full focus, but it was hard to concentrate with a horde of walking dead…undead?…unalive?…looming toward us.

I swiped my machete at the one who looked like Shade. The blade passed through his arm, but it didn't reform completely. A whisp of smoke lingered around the contact point, vibrating and fading as if it didn't have enough energy to turn solid.

I gasped as the memory returned. "Servitors."

Discord frowned. "Was that supposed to be a spell?"

"It's a being Ash told me about. She said if she ever turned to dark magic, we'd know because she'd create a servitor to organize the library for her. I think she meant a tulpa."

"How does that piece of information help us now?"

The Mayhem tulpa struck out, slashing his claws against Discord's face. My demon roared and shoved the entity, opening the circle enough for me to dart through. My coven and the damn centaur followed me toward the pool while Discord's buddies stayed with him.

"If they're just part of Ruin's imagination, that means they aren't real."

Discord dodged a punch, shoving his other brother into the wall. "They're real enough to cause us bodily harm."

"Only because we believe they can hurt us." I stood still, my back to the pool, and faced my deepest fears and regrets head-on. My thoughts and emotions only had power over me because I gave it to them. It was time I took it back.

"I'd joked along with my sister and asked her to send the servitor my way when she was done with him. She said it would only work if I truly believed in it."

Discord snapped his gaze toward me. "Our imagination fuels them too."

"Bingo. Ash said the moment you stop believing in a thoughtform, it loses its ability to help...or in this case...hurt you."

The Mr. Beefy tulpa slammed a fist into Discord's stomach, making him double over. He straightened and threw a punch, but his arm passed right through the spine ripper's head.

Discord backpedaled three steps before he hit a wall. Six entities surrounded him, black smoke billowing around their feet as the faceless four began to fuse into his brothers' forms.

"What's the plan?" he asked

My heart galloped in my chest, and I sucked in a deep breath, centering myself. "Take back your power, stand there, and let them attack. They can't hurt you if you don't give them the ability to."

"Are you sure it will work?"

I straightened my spine and looked the Ash tulpa in the eyes. "I'm betting my life on it."

Hecate, have mercy. The entities attacked.

CHAPTER 20

DISCORD

I tried to do as Cinder instructed, to simply use disbelief to disarm my attackers, but with my powers bound and my confidence crushed, my attempt was futile. My brothers glared at me with venom in their gazes, heavy with accusations and premature triumph.

"Let us see you win a fair fight...without your precious amulet." Mayhem's lip curled into a sneer. "You're not so powerful now, brother."

Chaos struck, his fist sinking into my gut. I doubled over, and Mayhem landed an uppercut to my chin, whipping my head back, sharp pain exploding down my spine. Their punches certainly felt real enough, so how was I to convince myself they weren't?

I straightened, my vertebrae cracking as I stretched my neck. "No fight is fair when my powers are bound."

I threw a fist, clocking Mayhem in the jaw before he could turn to smoke. He lashed back, his arm turning demonic, his talons screeching across the wall as I ducked and lunged left.

"You talk of fairness." He spat at my feet. "You filled my pockets with hellhound treats and challenged me to a wrestling match with Cerberus to win the amulet. Does Lucifer know of your deceit?"

I clamped my mouth closed. No, Lucifer did not know I'd rigged the fight when I'd wagered the amulet, and I planned to keep it that way. The knowledge that I'd cheated would only add fuel to the hatred burning in his heart. And now that Ruin knew of my trickery, my desire to annihilate him compounded.

"Lucifer knows far more than you think," I lied. "Deceit is his favorite game, after all."

I'd dealt with many demons over the centuries who'd aspired to usurp me and take my place by the king's side. When Mayhem, my own brother, became so disgruntled that he challenged me weekly, I'd put a stop to his nonsense, making him appear weak, while obtaining the amulet had secured my place in the court.

But I'd grown too powerful, unmatched by all except Lucifer and the goddess. Magic had aided my every whim until I no longer had to fight for anything. Perhaps that was why I'd allowed Isabel to seduce me, to trick me. I'd longed for something other than abso-lute power.

And in doing so, I had lost it all. Cinder was right. It was time I took it back. Not the amulet's false ampli-fication, but my own power within. The devil may have stripped my magic, but I would never allow anyone to take my mind.

Still, my heart pounded, doubt worming through my resolve. I tried to focus, recalling Cinder's words. The reality Ruin had created here was merely a suggestion.

I drew in a ragged breath, the ache of every blow I'd received settling into my bones. But beneath the pain, a spark ignited—a reminder of who I was before the amulet's allure, and I refused to let Ruin see doubt flicker in my eyes.

Instead, I straightened my shoulders, letting defi-ance hold my posture steady. Power was more than magic and trinkets, and I had survived worse than this. If I was to reclaim my strength, I would have to start here, with nothing but grit and resolve.

"You will never make it out of this alive, brother," the Chaos tulpa said. "Surrender now and save your-self the humiliation of pleading for your life in front of your little witch."

I glanced at Cinder in the distance. She stood near the pool alone, watching me, already triumphant over

Ruin's creations. Lifting her palms toward me, she mouthed the words *they're not real.*

But *she* was, as was I, and I would never succumb to defeat as long as my witch needed me.

I narrowed my eyes, my nostrils flaring. "You are no brother to me, Ruin. And your creations aren't real."

The Chaos tulpa laughed. "No? *This* isn't real?"

Mayhem struck from behind, jabbing his talons into my back and twisting them, puncturing my lung. I gasped and sputtered as sharp, electrical pain ricocheted through my body, and I cut my gaze to Cinder. Concern furrowed her brow, and she shook her head, but she offered no assistance.

Mayhem removed his claws from my abdomen, and Chaos landed another punch to my gut. I dragged in another breath, focusing on the pain in my lung, willing my body to heal.

"You're a coward," I rasped. "Even Bedlam had the boldness to fight me himself."

I lashed out an arm, but it passed through smoke. Mayhem backhanded the side of my skull, knocking me off my feet. Chaos lunged, dropping to his knees and gripping my throat, pinning me to the floor. His other hand morphed, talons extending from his fingertips as he raised his arm, ready to take out my heart. Mayhem loomed behind him, his sinister smile revealing too many teeth.

"Now is not the time for a nap, silly." Cinder's voice cut through the madness, and I focused my wavering vision on her silhouette moving toward me. "Are you going to lie there all day, or can we get moving?"

"I'm a bit preoccupied." I forced the words through my crushed throat.

"With what? A bedtime story?" She rested her hands on her hips, shifting her weight to one leg. "Get up."

"I can't." Chaos gripped me harder, his muscles coiling in his arm.

"Why not?" She looked at me as if I'd grown a second set of horns. "There's nothing holding you down. Nothing *real*."

Nothing... I looked at Chaos. "You can't hurt me."

"Watch me." He plunged his talons toward my heart. The tips pierced my skin.

I closed my eyes, inhaling deeply and focusing on Cinder's words. These tulpas were not my brothers. Chaos, as ornery as he was, would never wish me dead, so this being was simply a fabrication.

And I refused to give it any more power.

I opened my eyes to find confusion morphing both their faces. The Chaos tulpa's talons should have been embedded in my heart, yet only a whisp of smoke floated atop my chest.

Cinder stretched out her arm, and I accepted the gesture, allowing her to help me to my feet. I passed through the tulpa as if walking through a fog and took my witch into my arms.

"Your mind never ceases to amaze me." I pressed a kiss to the top of her head.

She drew in a breath to respond when the air around us crackled. The tulpas dissolved into smoke, the last echoes of their voices fading like laughter down a long hall. Then, silence.

Once again, too still. Too quiet.

"Cinder," I said, scanning the shadows, Ruin's energy vibrating around us. "Stay behind me."

"Not a chance." She lifted her chin. "If he's finally done hiding, I want front-row seats."

A rumble shook the ground, deep and guttural. The walls warped, and the air thickened until the pressure made my ears pop. The remaining smoke congealed into a mass of writhing shadow, limbs unfurling, eyes—hundreds of them—blinking open one by one.

"Ah," came the haunting voice, smooth and mocking. "The prodigal prince and his little flame. You've made quite the mess of my garden."

"Enough tricks," I said. "Face me as a demon, not a shadow."

"As you wish." Ruin stepped from the darkness, his true form towering, more nightmare than flesh. His skin glistened like liquid obsidian, veins of red light pulsing beneath. Horns coiled backward like a ram's, and his grin was more sinister than I'd ever seen.

He lunged.

I met him head-on, hellfire igniting in my fists. His claws scraped against my forearm, splitting skin as I shoved him back, the impact rattling my bones. He countered, landing a blow that sent me skidding across the floor.

"Discord!" Cinder's voice cut through the haze. She hurled a ball of witch fire, searing the air between us. It struck Ruin square in the chest, but he only laughed as the flames slid across his skin.

"An admirable attempt," he said, "but your mortal tricks don't work here."

"I can do a lot more than put on a smoke show." Cinder smirked. "Can you?"

I rose and stepped forward, placing myself between them. "You were always more bark than bite, Ruin."

He laughed, rows of fangs glinting like daggers as he towered above us, a mass of slick muscle and molten veins. "I've missed this," he said, and he inhaled deeply. "The smell of fear."

I growled low in my throat, loath to admit it wasn't just Cinder's fear tainting the air...it was also my own. My body ached, bruised and beaten. My lung had barely healed, and the rips in my flesh stung as if filled with salt and spirits. Alone and in my weakened state, I was no match for the fiend standing before me.

But I wasn't alone. Not anymore.

Ruin lunged. I tried to dodge his advance, my shoulder taking the brunt of the hit as I crashed to the floor. My ribs protested. Breathing hurt. Everything hurt. He was stronger, faster, and I was trapped in this damned human shell.

He caught me by the throat and lifted me like I weighed nothing. "You're weak, Discord. Defanged. Declawed. Reduced to a man."

"Maybe," I rasped, "but you should know better than to underestimate a man with something to lose."

Cinder hurled another fireball, hitting him in the side of the head.

"Pathetic," he said, turning toward her. "Did your little prince not teach you that witch fire doesn't hurt demons?"

"It might not hurt," she said, arching a brow, "but it does distract."

I wrenched free, sucking air through my bruised windpipe and plunging my knife into his side.

He jerked it out, sneering as his taloned hand heated, glowing first blue, then white, melting the blade and disintegrating the handle. "You'll both die screaming."

"You first," Cinder said, her eyes narrowing before

she looked at me and tilted her head, mouthing the words *what's the plan?*

I raised my brows, hoping to convey that I was working on it, though my thoughts currently bounced between agony and profanity. Then I remembered what lay behind Ruin. I jerked my head, and she followed my gaze before looking into my eyes and nodding.

No hesitation. No question. The plan was in place, and we only had to execute it.

Ruin swung. The wind of it alone sent dust spinning around our feet. Cinder ducked, skidding beneath his arm and slicing her knife across the back of his knee. He roared, lashing out. I moved in from the other side, slamming into him with everything I had left. It felt as if I were tackling a wall of fire and iron.

He backhanded me, and the world went sideways. My head hit stone. Warmth trickled down my neck. Through the blur, I saw Cinder still standing, her chest heaving but her spine straight.

"Your soul will taste divine," Ruin hissed.

She smiled faintly. "Funny. I was about to say the same."

He lunged at her, his forearm hitting the side of her head, knocking her to the ground. Her skull hit the ground with a sickening crack, and she fell limp at his feet.

Panic flushed my veins, frigid and sharp, and

instinct took over. I called on what little power I had left, forcing myself to my feet.

Ruin lifted a taloned foot above her head, his muscles coiling, ready to crush her. I plowed toward him, dropping and sliding across the ground to retrieve Cinder's knife. I rolled and shot to my feet once more, slashing the blade across the back of his heel, severing the tendon.

He wailed and stumbled back. Cinder groaned, lifting her head and blinking repeatedly. I allowed myself to feel a moment of relief as my witch rose to her feet, but we had no time to waste. The injury I'd caused Ruin would heal in seconds.

Cinder threw a massive fireball, the air heating as it flashed passed me and slammed into Ruin's chest. The impact knocked him off balance, and he stumbled again. The energy in the chamber thickened, vibrating and sharpening. I didn't dare turn around to witness the tulpa forming behind me.

"Your monsters can't hurt us anymore." Cinder crossed her arms as the shadow closed in around her.

My pulse sprinted, my stomach souring at the sight of darkness attempting to devour the woman I loved. But she held strong to her disbelief, and the thoughtform passed through her.

I hurled the knife, and it spun pommel over tip before sinking into Ruin's shoulder. Cinder lunged, her arms outstretched, and pushed him backward, to the edge of the pool. His foot slipped on the ledge, his taloned toes dipping into the purple liquid before he caught his balance.

The entities trapped inside reached upward, their gnarled hands breaking the surface and latching onto his ankles.

Ruin froze, recognition flashing in his molten eyes. "No—"

"Say hello to your little friends," Cinder said, and together, we shoved. He teetered, his claws scraping stone, his expression one of sheer terror.

"How do you like the smell of fear now?" I asked.

He tumbled backward into the pool. The purple liquid swallowed him whole, and for one heartbeat, all was silent.

Then the water exploded with motion.

Hundreds of hands, spectral and skeletal, shot upward, clawing at him. They wrapped around his horns, his limbs, his throat. His scream echoed through the chamber as they dragged him into their depths. The last thing I saw before the surface closed over him was his face, twisted in rage and terror as the souls he'd tortured claimed their revenge.

The pool went still. Cinder and I stood side by side, panting, staring into the silence that followed.

She rested a hand on my biceps. "Think he'll come back from that?"

I wiped blood from my mouth. "I doubt those souls will ever let him go."

She let out a shaky laugh, brushing a lock of hair from her face. "Good. Because I am *so* done with demons for the day."

The ground shook, and cracks splintered up the wall. Cinder's eyes widened, and for a moment, neither of us moved. A fissure formed in the wall, veins pulsing around the crack as it widened.

"Seriously." Cinder widened her stance. "No more demons today."

Bright light spilled through the opening—not Hell's orange moonlight, but something colder. Paler. Silver. It pulsed like a heartbeat, slow and steady, raising the vibration in the chamber and making my arm hairs stand on end.

Cinder clutched my hand. "Do you think that's...?"

I nodded once. "Indeed."

We had defeated Ruin.

But our confrontation with the goddess had just begun.

CHAPTER 21

DISCORD

"Are you ready?" Cinder squeezed my hand.

I laughed dryly. Was I ready to face the goddess of magic, whose wrath would likely tear me to shreds the moment her gaze met mine? "No, not really."

We stepped through the fissure, and the heat of Ruin's chamber vanished behind us, chilling stillness replacing it. The silver light dimmed to a soft glow, illuminating an endless cavern carved of obsidian and bone. The air smelled of frost and rot, an impossible combination that made my skin crawl.

Then, I saw her.

Hecate hung suspended above a black altar, her body bound in chains that glowed faintly with demonic sigils. Her long, silver hair drifted like smoke on a breeze, her eyes half-lidded but aware. Even broken, she radiated power, the kind that humbles you without words.

"Holy Hec..." Cinder trailed off, her voice a whisper. "Is that...?"

"Yes," I said quietly. "The goddess herself."

Cinder started forward, her steps echoing across the stone. "We have to help her."

"Careful," I warned. "Those chains were forged for deities. Touch the wrong rune, and it could melt you from the inside out."

"Just like in *Indiana Jones*," she said.

We approached the altar, and the chains hummed, reacting to our presence. I could feel Ruin's magic woven through them—layered, precise, merciless. This was no simple prison. It was meant to drain her.

"Cinder," Hecate's voice rasped, barely audible yet filled with divine resonance. "You came."

Cinder froze. "You know who I am?"

"Your mother told me about you and your sisters." She closed her eyes and let out a long hiss, as if speaking pained her.

Tears welled in Cinder's eyes. "She's alive? And my dad?"

"I helped them escape." The goddess wheezed and opened her eyes. "As you will now help me."

Cinder brought a trembling hand to her lips. "Where are they?"

Hecate hissed again, her eyes rolling upward until only the whites were visible.

"Enough questions. We must release her." I circled the altar, examining the chains. "Ruin tied the binds to her essence...a trick he learned from Lucifer. If we break them the wrong way, we might kill her."

"Then we find the right way," Cinder said, her voice steady, filled with resolve. "Nothing is impossible. Not if we think it through."

Her determination sparked something in me. For centuries, I'd lived in a world where power was brute force, where thinking too long was a weakness. But Cinder made intellect feel like defiance.

"Alright," I said. "We outthink the bastard."

I hovered my hand above the nearest chain, just shy of touching it, and the sigils pulsed red. I closed my eyes, reaching out with my mind and tracing the flow of energy. The bindings were a circuit, using darkness to feed on the goddess's power. If we could disrupt the current with light...

"Cinder, channel your firelight into the binding sigil on the shackle here." I pointed to Hecate's wrist. "Slow and steady. Focus on your light rather than heat."

My witch nodded, unquestioning, and held her hand toward the shackle. Her flames flickered gold rather than red, as soft as candlelight. The binding sigil glowed, growing brighter and brighter, its low vibration fighting against Cinder's high. Then it faltered, and the chain shuddered.

"That's it," I whispered. "You're burning the darkness out."

She bit her lip, focusing, sweat beading on her forehead. The first chain snapped, the sound echoing through the cavern like a scream before dissolving into smoke. Hecate's arm dropped, hanging limp at her side as her expression contorted into one of pure agony.

"Oh, Goddess. I'm so sorry." Cinder wrung her hands. "It's hurting her."

"But it's working." I squeezed her shoulders. "Try the next one."

"Which one?" Her gaze bounced from the goddess's arm to her ankles.

"What feels right?" I asked, sending a pulse of magic into my witch, bringing clarity to her thoughts.

"None of them." She shook her head, and I released her.

"Help me," Hecate rasped.

"Just choose one." I stepped away, giving Cinder room to work.

"Okay, I'll try the opposite ankle." She lit another soft flame and sent it into the shackle.

Hecate mumbled something inaudible. Her head jerked back, and drool ran from the corner of her mouth. Cinder cringed, her brow crumpling as she poured her light into the second shackle. Her breathing grew shallow with her exertion, but she continued feeding her light into the darkness until the sigil popped and the bind dissolved.

Hecate wailed in pain.

Cinder shook her hands. "This isn't right. She'll die if we keep doing this."

"What else can we do?" I asked.

"I don't know."

I grasped her shoulders once more and sent a wave of magic into her psyche. She gasped, her eyes glazing, and through our bond, I felt her connect with the goddess's mind. The sheer power of her light nearly knocked me from my feet.

I closed my eyes, focusing only on my soulbride, my magic, my essence mingling with hers until I couldn't tell where I ended and she began. Light and dark, high and low, evil and goodness mixing and melding, creating a symphony of indisputable power.

"Her heart!" Cinder's voice brought me back to myself, and I released her. She climbed onto the altar, her hands trembling above the goddess's chest. "We have to break the heart bind. Come here."

I joined her atop the stone table. "Tell me what to do."

"Exactly what you just did." She took my hand in hers and hovered her other over Hecate's heart. Lighting a soft golden flame, she focused her intent on freeing the goddess and opened herself to me once more.

Our magic melded instantly, as if it were two halves of the same whole, and my skin turned to gooseflesh. Cinder's high vibration hummed in my muscles, making them twitch as she used my essence to fuel her own and focused it into the invisible chain.

Searing pain lanced through me as the bind fought back, and I absorbed it, channeling it away from Cinder so she could continue her work unhindered. Her palm heated, slick with sweat, and a prickling sensation shot up my arm, igniting in my chest.

Hecate groaned. Cinder wheezed. An earth-shattering snap echoed through the chamber.

The shackles dissolved, and Hecate fell to her knees on the altar. I caught her arm before she could tumble to the ground, and an electric jolt ricocheted through my body, setting every nerve ablaze.

"You dare touch me?" The goddess yanked from my grasp and floated to the floor, her hair whipping in an invisible wind.

I slid from the table and lowered to one knee, casting my gaze to her feet. "My sincerest apologies, goddess. I am sorry...for everything. I knew not what the amulet meant when I wagered it."

I dared to look at her. White flames flickered in her silver eyes, and vibrating energy gathered around her, making my body itch.

"I will return it to you," I said. "You have my word."

"Please, goddess." Cinder pressed her palms together and bowed. "My sisters are searching for it as we speak. We will make things right."

Hecate straightened her spine on a quick inhale, her fury dimming to a simmer. "Do you have any idea what you've done?"

"I know." Cinder dropped her arms at her sides. "We've unraveled the veil by freeing Discord and his brothers, but we intend to fix it. We'll do whatever it takes."

The goddess scoffed. "You speak of 'we' as if you share the burden."

"We do," I said.

"Not you." Hecate glared at me, and I clamped my mouth shut.

"I..." Cinder swallowed hard. "It's my fault. I set it all in motion when I summoned Discord. The burden is mine to bear."

Hecate laughed, disbelieving. "Have you learned nothing, child? Your mother started this when she summoned Lucifer himself and used your father as her accomplice. If fate had not already woven your tale, I'd strike you both down here and now."

"My tale?" Cinder's voice cracked.

"Yours, your sisters'..." She waved a dismissive hand at me. "Theirs. You're meant to break the mold, unite the people, usher in an era of peace between the realms." Hecate steepled her fingers, and the invisible wind blowing through her hair quieted. "But you've torn the veil to shreds. Yes, it is your burden, but it's also your parents', your sisters', and theirs."

Again, she merely waved in my direction, which I supposed I should be grateful for. I deserved much worse than her casual disrespect.

"I never should have done this alone." Cinder clasped her hands together. "I know that now."

Hecate inclined her chin. "So you can learn. Good, because your strife isn't over yet. I released your parents from Lucifer's clutches, and they got away before his minions trapped me. Scorsha has been channeling my energy, attempting to hold the veil together while you searched for me and your sisters searched for my amulet. Your entire family, working together."

"Where are they?" Cinder asked, her voice quiet. "May I see them?"

"To find them, you have one more obstacle to over-come." The goddess raised her arms, and silver smoke billowed at her feet. It swirled upward, encasing her in fog before an intense light flashed, blinding me for a moment. When I opened my eyes, Cinder and I stood in the chamber alone.

"What obstacle?" Cinder rubbed her eyes and turned in a circle. "For eff's sake, what obstacle?"

She jabbed her fingers into her hair, pulling it at the roots, her frustration palpable. "And not so much as a thank you? What the hell?"

She dropped her arms at her sides. "That didn't go at all like I planned."

"I can take you to your parents." A gust of frigid air swept through the cavern, carrying the voice and the faint sound of footsteps.

I turned, instincts screaming. A shadow slipped through the fissure behind us—tall, graceful, deadly.

Seraphine.

She was fully healed, and her hair gleamed under the silver light, her eyes as cold as crystal. "I see the pitiful little fire witch found her goddess."

"Stay back," I warned, stepping in front of Cinder.

Seraphine ignored me, her gaze fixed on my soul-bride. "I never expected you to get this far, even after you threw me into the acid river."

Cinder curled her hands, sparks dancing across her palms. "You said you can take me to my parents."

Seraphine strolled toward us. "I did say that, didn't I?"

"She lies." I wound my arm back, hellfire igniting in my hand, but Cinder grabbed my wrist.

"She doesn't have to lie." She gave me a squeeze. "Does she?"

I opened myself to her, giving her what little

energy I had left, and she sent a pulse toward Seraphine.

"You made it this far. Why should I lie?" the insolent witch said. "I know where they're hiding. I've only let them live this long so I could see my mother's curse finally come to fruition."

"Your mother's?" Cinder gaped, blinking rapidly as she shook her head in disbelief.

"You are Isabel's firstborn." My brow slammed down over my eyes, a newfound fury sparking in my being.

"The soul she promised to you in exchange for cursing the Holland bloodline..." She sneered. "In the flesh."

"Where are my parents?" Cinder asked through clenched teeth, her waning magic pulsing one last time.

Seraphine held out her hand. "I'll take you to them."

My gut twisted. "Cinder, don't."

"She isn't lying. She can't be." My witch stepped around me.

"She will take you to them, but you may not survive the journey." I clutched her hand, holding her back, but she tugged from my grasp.

"You're smarter than you look, demon-boy." Seraphine raised her arm and made a twisting motion with her hand. Wind swirled at Cinder's feet, picking up debris as it rose around her.

"Enough," I snarled. "You're not taking her."

Seraphine's gaze slid to me. "She isn't yours to keep."

Before I could move, she fisted her hand and power rippled through the chamber. I staggered back as the swirling force wrapped around Cinder, lifting her from the ground, and her eyes met mine, wide and terrified.

"Discord!" she shouted, reaching for me.

I lunged, catching her hand for the briefest second before the tornado engulfed her. Her fingers slipped from mine as Seraphine ripped her away, pulling her through the fissure in a blinding flash of blue light.

I gave chase, darting through after them, my feet pounding the ground as I crossed the underground chamber and raced up the staircase and out of the shed. Orange moonlight illuminated the garden, casting long shadows across the rocky ground, but the atmosphere was still. Not a trace of the foul air witch or my soulbride remained.

The entire world fell quiet.

I sank to my knees, staring straight ahead, my heart hollow and burning, the silence pressing in like a vise. A guttural roar ripped from my chest, aching, anguished, piercing the quiet as hellfire burned hotter in my being than it ever had before.

When I finished, I sucked in a ragged breath and

Hecate's voice came softly beside me, "You're at a crossroads, demon. In my domain."

"What are my choices?" Pressure built in the back of my eyes.

"You took what was mine, so I've allowed yours to be taken. I will return to Lucifer, and you can reclaim your place by his side. Command his army as the veil crumbles and enjoy power beyond comprehension."

I scoffed but said nothing, awaiting her alternative. "Or continue your quest in your weakened state. Find your soulbride, if she's still alive, and face Lucifer from the opposing side, fighting with the mortals, completely stripped of your power."

My hands curled into fists. "I prefer what's behind door number three."

"And what is that?"

A sinister smile curved my lips as I rose to my feet. "You've picked the wrong demon to challenge, goddess."

Hell held its breath.

The saga continues in Desiring Discord...

ALSO BY CARRIE PULKINEN

Fire Witches of Salem Series

Chaos and Ash

Commanding Chaos

Claiming Chaos

Mayhem and Ember

Mending Mayhem

Mastering Mayhem

Discord and Cinder

Demanding Discord

Desiring Discord

Collection One: Books 1-3

Collection Two: Books 4-6

Collection Three: Books 7-9

New Orleans Nocturnes Series

License to Bite

Shift Happens

Life's a Witch

Santa Got Run Over by a Vampire

Finders Reapers

Swipe Right to Bite

Batshift Crazy

Holy Shift

Collection One: Books 1-3

Collection Two: Books 4-7

Crescent City Wolf Pack Series

Werewolves Only

Beneath a Blue Moon

Bound by Blood

A Deal with Death

A Song to Remember

Shifting Fate

Collection One: Books 1-3

Collection Two: Books 4-6

Haunted Ever After Series

Love at First Haunt

Second Chance Spirit

Third Time's a Ghost

Love and Ghosts

Love and Omens

Love and Curses

Collection One: Books 1 - 3

Collection Two: Books 4 - 6

Lessons in Divine Disasters

How to Steal a God's Heart

How to Flirt With the Angel of Death

How to Woo the World's First Vampire

Stand Alone Books

Flipping the Bird

The Rest of Forever

Soul Catchers

Bewitching the Vampire

ABOUT THE AUTHOR

Carrie Pulkinen is a paranormal romance author who has always been fascinated with things that go bump in the night. Of course, when you grow up next door to a cemetery, the dead (and the undead) are hard to ignore. Pair that with her passion for writing and her love of a good happily-ever-after, and becoming a paranormal romance author seems like the only logical career choice.

Before she decided to turn her love of the written word into a career, Carrie spent the first part of her professional life as a high school journalism and yearbook teacher. She loves good chocolate and bad puns, and in her free time, she likes to dance, drink wine, and travel with her family.

Connect with Carrie online:
CarriePulkinen.com